Penguin Books

I FOR ISOBEL

Amy Witting was born in Annandale, an inner suburb
of Sydney, in 1918. She attended Sydney University,
then taught French and English in State schools. She
has published one novel, *The Visit* (Nelson, 1977),
a book of verse, *Travel Diary* (Woodbine Press, 1985)
as well as numerous poems and short stories in
magazines such as *Quadrant* and the *New Yorker*.

I FOR ISOBEL

Amy Witting

PENGUIN BOOKS
Assisted by the Literature Board of the Australia Council

Penguin Books Australia Ltd
487 Maroondah Highway, PO Box 257
Ringwood, Victoria, 3134, Australia
Penguin Books Ltd
Harmondsworth, Middlesex, England
Viking Penguin Inc.
40 West 23rd Street, New York, NY 10010, USA
Penguin Books Canada Limited
2801 John Street, Markham, Ontario, Canada, L3R 1B4
Penguin Books (N.Z.) Ltd
182–190 Wairau Road, Auckland 10, New Zealand

First published by Penguin Books Australia, 1989

Copyright © Amy Witting, 1989

All Rights Reserved. Without limiting the rights under copyright
reserved above, no part of this publication may be reproduced,
stored in or introduced into a retrieval system, or transmitted,
in any form or by any means (electronic, mechanical, photocopying,
recording or otherwise), without the prior written permission
of both the copyright owner and the above publisher of this book.

Typeset in 11/13 Baskerville by Midland Typesetters, Maryborough
Made and printed in Australia by Australian Print Group, Maryborough

CIP

Witting, Amy, 1918–
I for Isobel.

ISBN 0 14 012624 4.

I. Title.

A823′.3

I FOR ISOBEL

CONTENTS

·

1 · The Birthday Present

A week before Isobel Callaghan's ninth birthday, her mother said, in a tone of mild regret, 'No birthday presents this year! We have to be very careful about money this year.'

Every year at this time she said this; every year Isobel chose not to believe it. Her mother was just saying that, she told herself, to make the present more of a surprise. Experience told her that there would be no present. As soon as they stepped out of the ferry onto the creaking wharf and set out for Mrs Terry's lakeside boarding house, where they spent the summer holidays, the flat reedy shore, the great Moreton Bay fig whose branches scaffolded the air of the boarding-house garden, the weed-bearded tennis court and the cane chairs with their faded flabby cushions, all spoke to Isobel of desolate past birthdays, but she did not believe experience, either. Day by day she watched for a mysterious shopping trip across the lake, for in the village there was only one tiny store which served as a post office too; when no mysterious journey took place, she told herself they must have brought the present secretly from home. Even on the presentless morning she would not give up hope entirely, but would search in drawers, behind doors, under beds, as if birthday presents were supposed to be hidden, like Easter eggs in the grass.

Mrs Callaghan, too, kept the birthday in mind and spoke of it now and then.

'January,' she said, 'is too close to Christmas for birthday presents,' and later, serenely, 'It is vulgar to celebrate birthdays away from home.'

Whenever she found a new argument against birthday presents for Isobel, a strange look of relief would appear on her face, and Isobel would be forced to accept, for the moment, that there would be no present.

Well, this year she would remember. This year, one week before Margaret's birthday, she would remember to say, in her mother's own tone, 'No birthday presents this year!' and see what they would make of that. But she knew, even as she muttered bitterly to herself, that she would not remember. She had no grasp of the calendar yet; holidays surprised her and the seasons were not attached to the names of months. Only Christmas could be foreseen, because of the decorations and Santa Claus in the shops. She got presents at Christmas, being lucky enough to have Christmas the same day as everyone else. Margaret's birthday, with the present – the real present wrapped in paper – was a black day for Isobel, but it always came without warning. It was not talked about beforehand, like her own.

This year, the day before the birthday, her mother said in her real voice, 'Now, Isobel, you are not to go about tomorrow telling people it's your birthday. I could have died of shame last year, with you running about like a little beggar telling everyone it was your birthday. We don't want any more behaviour of that kind.'

Last year she had disgraced the family, that was true. On a giddy impulse she had run into the garden among the deckchairs, shouting, 'It's my birthday! Today is my birthday!' Skinny, crinkled Mr Daubeney had shouted back,

'Catch this then!' and spun a two-shilling piece in the air.
She had caught it in the lap of her skirt – she hadn't had
time to begin to be clumsy – and somebody else had cried
out, 'Here's another!' 'Over here!' 'Here you are, Isobel!'
She had held up her skirt like a pouch and had caught
all the coins, spinning round and laughing, and the grown-
ups were laughing too, as she called out, 'Thank you very
much!' and ran inside with her treasure.

Her mother was standing watching inside the long glass
door of the bedroom. She dug her fingers into Isobel's arm
and hissed, 'Let your skirt down! Let it down!' She took
the coins Isobel had gathered, stared at them in her hand
and moaned, 'Asking for money, asking for money. How
could you shame me like this?' When her father came in,
her mother pointed to the money and said, 'She's been going
about begging for money, telling everyone it's her birthday.
Oh, what shall we do? Can we give it back?'

Isobel was sitting on the bed, not allowed to go out in
case she disgraced the family again, and subdued because
her mother was too upset even to be angry.

'Can you remember who gave it to you?'

She shook her head.

Her father said, sounding tired, 'I don't think we had
better say any more about it. You mustn't ask people for
money, you know, Isobel.'

Last year, the day had been terrible, and the worst thing
about it was that the lovely moment of the spinning coins
and the laughing voices had turned out to be bad behaviour.
Thinking about it, she wondered what had become of the
money, but that didn't matter very much. The money had
been real treasure when it was flying through the air – after
that it had been only a cause of shame.

She forgot about last year when the meaning of her
mother's words sank in, that she was not to tell, not to
tell anyone that it was her birthday. She was by nature

timid, anxious only to know what was required of her so as to keep out of trouble, but she didn't think she could do that. It was like being asked to walk into a crack in the wall – it was just not possible.

Now she was sure there would be no present. Tomorrow morning she would not look, and that was a step towards the kind of person she longed to be but did not have words to describe – someone safe behind a wall of her own building.

But not to tell, not to say just once, 'It's my birthday today!' She thought, I shall tell the tree. She saw herself hiding her face between two sharp folds of the tree trunk and whispering, 'It's my birthday today,' and felt a thrilling pain in her tight throat, as if she was reading *The Little Match Girl* in the old book of fairytales at Auntie Ann's.

That put her in a reading mood. She went into the lounge, where there were bookshelves full of books for guests, with a special shelf for children's books. She had read that out long ago; she looked through it but there was nothing new and nothing she wanted to read again, so she began to look through the other shelves. She took out a book called *The Adventures of Sherlock Holmes*, thinking that adventures could never be dull, read the first sentence, *To Sherlock Holmes she is always* the *woman*, and was disappointed – that didn't sould like the beginning of an adventure. She turned to the next story, *A Case of Identity:*

'My dear fellow,' said Sherlock Holmes, as we sat on either side of the fire in his lodgings at Baker Street, 'life is infinitely stranger than anything which the mind of man could invent. We would not dare to conceive the things which are really mere commonplaces of existence. If we could fly out of that window hand in hand, hover over this great city, gently remove the roofs, and peep in at the queer things which are going on . . .'

Birthdays, injustices, parents all vanished. She sat on the

floor reading till the noise of cups and saucers in the kitchen warned her that the grown-ups would be coming in for afternoon tea, then she went to the little room where she and Margaret slept, next to their parents' bedroom. It was too hot there, but if she went outside to the cool shade of the fig tree, Caroline and Joanne Mansell would come asking her to play with them, or Margaret would want her to go for a swim. Besides, it wasn't hot in Baker Street.

What a lucky thing that she had found this new place in time to spend the birthday there. Presents didn't matter so much, if life had these enchanting surprises that were free to everyone.

She read without stirring until Margaret came in and said, 'Mum says you're to wash your hands before dinner.'

Dinner was the meal which at home they called tea. Mrs Callaghan pronounced the word with a conscious elegance which Margaret imitated, maddening Isobel, who was about to hiss, 'Tea!' but recollected herself and said, 'Can I have the light on for a while tonight?'

'We're not allowed to read in bed.'

'Oh go on, don't be mean. It's different on holidays. It's only at home that we aren't allowed to read in bed.'

'You ask them then.'

Isobel hid the book under her pillow.

'Ho, ho.' Margaret spoke with adult poise, then relented with adult satisfaction. 'Oh, all right. So long as you put it out before they come to bed. They can see the light under the door, you know. And go and wash your hands because I was told to tell you.'

Isobel went quietly, because of Margaret's kindness about the light.

The birthday still cast its shadow, in spite of Holmes and Watson. While she ate her tea, she was thinking how wonderful it would be if beside her bed in the morning she found a huge box wrapped in paper, with a big bow and a card that said HAPPY BIRTHDAY ISOBEL. She would try to lift it but it would be too heavy, so she would rip away the paper and lift the lid, and there would be THE COMPLETE WORKS OF ARTHUR CONAN DOYLE, books and books and books. It was a lovely dream, but then she woke up to reality and felt the worse for it.

After tea she had to play Snap with Margaret and the Mansell girls while she thought about Holmes and Watson and longed to go to bed and read. Bed time came at last and was wonderful; Margaret went to sleep straight away, so she put her clothes on the floor in front of the crack at the bottom of the door and read until she was nearly asleep and could just stay awake long enough to put out the light.

She woke early and thought at once, with tightened heart, 'Don't look. It isn't any use.' Then she remembered the tree ceremony, which she had better perform before anyone else was up. Quickly she put on yesterday's clothes and ran outside to the fig tree, but when she reached it she saw a pair of legs dangling and there was Caroline, sitting on a low branch looking down at her.

'You're up early.'

Isobel wanted to say, 'So are you,' but other words were too pressing on her tongue. She said instead, 'Can I tell you a secret? You're not to tell anyone else.'

Caroline's eyes lit with interest. 'Sure. Go on.'

'It's my birthday today.'

'That's not a secret.' Caroline was disappointed and resentful. 'Birthdays aren't secrets. Not ever.'

'Well, mine is. How do you know, anyhow? Plenty of people might have secret birthdays and you don't know because they are secret.'

'I don't see why.' Caroline buttoned her lips and shook her head firmly, so that her fat fair plaits swung wide.

'Well, people have secret weddings, I know that much.

In books they have them often. And if you were a baby and you weren't supposed to be born, so you were smuggled away to somebody else, then nobody would know your birthday, so it would be a secret, wouldn't it? What about Moses? I bet nobody knew his birthday.'

Caroline didn't intend to tangle with Moses. She knew less about the content of books than Isobel, but she knew the world better. She said with authority, 'Somebody always knows.' Then she dropped down from the branch, saying, 'I think I'll go and see if Joanne's awake. See you later, alligator.' Sauntering across the grass, she turned her head and called, recklessly loud, 'Many happy returns!'

Isobel would have done better to tell the tree.

She went back to fetch her book, having another celebration in mind – a mean, private one. She was going to hide from her parents until breakfast time, so that if they wanted to wish her a happy birthday they could do it in front of everyone. Or if they liked, they could forget it. All the better if they did – she hated the way they searched her face for signs of sulking, so that they could laugh and say, 'What a long face on your birthday!' 'Frown on your birthday, frown all year!', knowing perfectly well that she was miserable because she hadn't got a present.

She felt sure they would be ashamed not to mention her birthday at all. There was going to be a little fun in this, if it worked.

Margaret had not stirred. Isobel took her book and crept out. With unusual forethought she washed her face and hands and even combed her hair, so there wouldn't be any trouble about that. Then she went to her hideyhole, the big old chair on the back verandah. The chair wasn't meant for sitting on; it faced the wall, there was stuffing coming out of it that prickled against her legs and it was lopsided because one leg was broken, but she could manage to curl up in it and be out of sight.

She read until the breakfast bell sounded, then waited a little longer before she sneaked through the kitchen. That was forbidden ground, but Mrs Terry and Irene, the waitress, were too busy to notice her.

The Mansells, father and mother and Caroline and Joanne, were there already, and Miss Halwood and old Mrs Halwood were coming in, so she was sitting calmly eating her Weetbix under powerful protection when her parents arrived.

'Well, there you are!' said her mother in a gentle, reasonable tone. 'Wherever have you been?'

'Just outside.'

Old Mr Welch coming in said, 'With her head in a book, I suppose. It's quite a bookworm you have there, Mrs Callaghan.'

Dangerous ground.

'What are you reading now, Isobel?' asked Miss Halwood, who was a teacher in real life.

Oh dear, the quicksand itself.

'*The Adventures of Sherlock Holmes.*'

'Goodness me,' said Mrs Halwood, 'that's a difficult book for a little girl.'

With thin saintliness, Mrs Callaghan said, 'You know you are not to take grown-up books without permission.'

'Oh, Mrs Callaghan,' said Miss Halwood, 'there is really nothing wrong with Sherlock Holmes.'

'A lot more moral than Biggles,' said Mr Welch.

'Besides,' went on Miss Halwood, 'it would be a shame to check her when she is so advanced. I only wish some of my pupils read so well.'

'Your poor sister is outside looking for you, Isobel,' her mother said. 'You had better go and find her.'

Isobel got up to go, but Margaret, coming through the door, said easily, 'I thought you must be in here,' and took her place.

'Do you understand all the words, Isobel?' Miss Halwood asked.

'I guess some of them.' Drunk on approval, she spoke with too much pride.

'That isn't a bad way of learning, but it's a good idea to look up one or two in the dictionary. Don't look up so many that you get bored with reading. That would be a pity.'

'I couldn't ever get bored with reading.'

'You're a lucky girl, then. I'm lucky too in the same way. The only reason I'd like to be your age again is to have all the wonderful books to read for the first time.'

'How old is she?' Mrs Halwood asked Mrs Callaghan.

Oh, oh. How do you like that, Mrs Callaghan? Isobel saw the red rising in her mother's face and dropped her eyes demurely. Margaret was staring with a puzzled look at her mother; her father was eating, paying no attention.

Mrs Callaghan said quietly, 'She is nine.'

'Remarkably advanced for her age,' said Miss Halwood.

Isobel was living in two worlds. Miss Halwood's, where she belonged and things were solid and predictable, and the other one, where she was exulting at making her mother uncomfortable. That was a great pleasure but it was like gobbling sweets – she expected some sickness from it. Meanwhile there was the world of Sherlock Holmes, which was better than both of them. She said, 'May I be excused, please?' and hurried back to her chair. She fished out the book from under the seat and went back to Baker Street.

She read until she had finished the book, then she went to the lounge to change it for *Further Adventures of Sherlock Holmes*, which she had seen on the shelf beside it. On the way back, she met her mother.

'I was looking for you, Isobel. I want you to go down to the shop and buy me a small writing pad.' She handed her a two-shilling piece, then added, smiling kindly, 'You may keep the change because it's your birthday.'

Well, her mother had wriggled her way out of that one, but not for nothing. Isobel took the coin and set off for the shop. She knew it was no fortune, yet there might be enough of it left to buy something that could be called a birthday present.

In the shop she asked for the smallest writing pad and put the coin on the counter.

'That will be one and elevenpence ha'penny,' said the shopkeeper. To her fallen face, he said, 'It's all right, girlie. You've got enough. You even get change, see.'

He handed her the kack-coloured insult. She took it and the writing pad and plunged out.

You couldn't make yourself safe, no matter how you tried. They could always surprise you. She wanted to hurl the coin into the water but she knew she mustn't express any feeling at all. 'Blessed Mary, Virgin Mother, make me not cry. I don't want to cry, Blessed Mary, Mother of God, baby Jesus, I don't want to cry. Help me, Blessed Mary, Virgin Mother, and baby Jesus . . .' If once she started to cry, she wouldn't be able to stop. 'I won't cry, I won't. Help me, Blessed Mary.'

At last, the prayer made a patch of candle-lit calm in her mind. She slowed and steadied, the need to cry having passed.

When she got back, the bedroom was empty. Perhaps Blessed Mary had seen to it that she didn't have to meet her mother straight away; Isobel found the special attention comforting. She murmured, 'Thank you, Blessed Mary,' left the writing pad and took her book. As for the repulsive halfpenny, she wanted to do something wicked and outrageous with it, but she lacked knowledge of the suitable curse.

She dropped it into one of the drawers. If they asked

her what she had done with it, she would say she had put it in the poor-box on the shop counter.

She went to the small room to leave her book on her bed. Margaret wasn't there – the lunch bell must have gone while she was out. She hurried to the dining room and sure enough, everyone else was at the table. Only her place was empty.

Except for a little parcel wrapped in pink tissue paper and tied with gold string. Keeping her eyes on it, she sat down warily.

Mr Mansell said at length, 'Aren't you going to open your parcel, Isobel?'

A harsh loud voice came out of her mouth, saying, 'Is that thing mine?'

She heard her mother draw in a long breath of rage and wondered why, but she did not look away from the little parcel.

'Yes,' said Mr Mansell, in a funny, slow, clear voice, like a teaching giving dictation, 'it is a present for you, for your birthday.'

With jumping fingers she untied, unwrapped, opened a little box. Pinned to a card which read on top *Elegance* and underneath *Fashion Jewellery* there was a gold brooch shaped like a basket, an old-fashioned one with a wide brim and a curly handle; there were coloured flowers in it, three little white bells with green tips, two daffodils, a pink rose and a blue flower with petals edged like a saw. It was beautiful. *It was a present for a real girl.*

How strange it was. Birthday after birthday she had hoped, and at last, after she had given up hope, the present had come, better than anything she could have imagined. She lifted it out of the box, set it on the lid and read it like a book while she ate her lunch.

Mrs Callaghan had recovered her company voice. 'How kind of you!'

'It's only a small thing,' said Mr Mansell.

'Oh, but you shouldn't have!' Chancing on a useful phrase in a foreign language, she said graciously, 'She's spoilt enough already!'

There was a disturbance – a kind of gust of breathing – at grown-up-face level round the table. Isobel looked up and saw that all the grown-ups were turning on her mother the same glare of indignation, except Mr Mansell, who was looking at Isobel herself with a bright, soft look that puzzled her, and her pale father, who was going steadily on with his task of cutting, chewing and swallowing. Her mother, for once, was even paler than he, so white-faced that traces of an earlier colouring showed russet in her hair and green in her eyes. She was staring at her plate, plying her knife and her fork slowly and carefully like crutches. Isobel felt an ache of sympathy, knowing how it felt to be the last to be chosen, or even left out of the game. Besides, what was wrong with what her mother had said? It sounded just like the stuff grown-ups usually talked.

She forgot sympathy in looking at her brooch. When she had finished eating, she put it back in its box, wrapped it, clutched it, gabbled, 'May I be excused, please?' and ran away to her room, where she sat on her bed, reading and looking from time to time at the brooch, unwrapping and wrapping it carefully each time.

The sound of her mother's quick, foreboding tread made her push the box in a panic under her pillow. Now, she remembered: she had been told not to tell, and she had told. She had told Caroline, who had told Mr Mansell, and retribution was coming, as her mother advanced with set face and luminous glare and began to slap her, muttering, 'Don't you dare to cry. Ungrateful little bitch. Don't–you–dare–to–cry. You little swine, thankless little swine, you couldn't say thank you, couldn't even say thank you.' Slap, slap. 'Don't open your mouth, don't you dare to cry.'

There was not much to cry about, for her mother's intentions were far more violent than her blows. Her hands flapped weakly as if she was fighting against a cage of air. She straightened up and drew breath. 'Mr Mansell rowed right across the lake to get you that brooch and you couldn't take the trouble to say thank you. It's no use going anywhere with you; you bring disgrace on us wherever we go. Ah, it's no use. Words are wasted on you, gawping there like an idiot.' She put her hands to her head and walked out in despair.

Isobel took the box from under the pillow, took out the brooch and looked at it while she rubbed her stinging legs. Why hadn't her mother taken the brooch? It would have been so easy. Isobel could even supply the words she had dreaded to hear: 'Give me that, you don't deserve to have it. Come on, give it to me.' Why hadn't she said them? Could it be that there were things her mother couldn't do?

That idea was too large to be coped with. She put it away from her, but she took the brooch and pinned it carefully to the neck of her dress. It was hers now, all right. She went and looked at it in the glass and stood admiring it. In one way or another, she would be wearing it all her life.

2 · False Idols and a Fireball

Isobel could honestly swear that she did see a fireball once. It was long ago, when she was quite small. Coming from school she was caught in a thrashing rainstorm and when she reached the house she found it locked and empty, so she was standing in the yard ankle-deep in water when the sky cracked and this pink ball came streaking past and then the water she was standing in turned rosy red. She could swear to that, although fireball became another word for lie and the rosy water was dammed up forever behind a wall of derisive laughter. In the days before she conquered enthusiasm she would sometimes come running in crying, 'Guess what I saw!' and her mother would say, 'A fireball?', sliding a glance of sophisticated amusement towards any other occupant of the room, for it was a well-known joke.

In another mood, Mrs Callaghan would say shortly, 'Thought you saw,' and sometimes she would hear Isobel out, then begin to question her: 'Where did this happen? When? What happened then? Now I thought you said . . .', ending always, 'You don't know, do you? You don't know whether you're telling the truth or not,' with a sigh of resignation.

It was well established that Isobel was a liar. When asked,

'Did you spend your mission money on chocolate, Isobel?'
she would say no, though she had, and Mrs Callaghan
would send a contemptuous knowing glance towards her
elder daughter Margaret, who had brought home the
information, while Margaret would look back with her
mouth sagging and her eyes full of misery, then turn on
Isobel the same look, a real blackout curtain of sorrow.
Isobel did not expect to be believed, but she felt that a
lie was the only contribution she could make to the
respectability of the occasion. She lived well enough herself
with her cowardice, her dishonesty and her greed, but others
had to be protected from the shock of them.

Meanwhile, fireballs existed and were seen even by liars,
and Isobel did not begin to worry seriously about truth
and falsehood until the day she forgot her composition
book and Sister Ignatius said she was not surprised. Looking
at Isobel and yet looking beyond her, her face pale and
her eyes dull, she said, frowning, 'You forget a lot of things,
Isobel Callaghan. Forget your school money, too, every
second week.' Isobel hadn't taken account of the number
of times she forgot her school money but the accusation
did not surprise her, for at home they had a wild beast
of poverty which broke loose now and then and filled the
air with screaming.

That afternoon she told her mother what Sister Ignatius
had said. Mrs Callaghan stared, then made her say it again;
after that, she turned her head away and uttered a dry, forced
whimper, like a small child determined to cry – a terrible
sound that carried conviction in spite of its obvious
affectation. She stopped that almost at once and began to
ask questions: 'Where were you? Who else was there? What
was her voice like, was it loud?'

Until then Isobel had been sincerely pleased with the
effect she was making, but she remembered suddenly the
usual end of such interrogations and she realised that to

tell the truth was not easy. Concentrating on the task of recalling the nun's voice to her mind, she took great care to describe it exactly.

'It was soft and tired and angry. It wasn't loud but I think everybody could hear it.'

Her mother sighed harshly. 'What's the use of asking you? Half the time you don't know what you're talking about.'

It was a strange thing that Isobel had heard that said so often and had taken no real notice of it before. This time she had made such an earnest effort to reach the truth, and in vain, that she felt sure all at once that the incident had not happened at all. She accepted herself as a hopeless born liar and wanted to cry out against being believed this time. What would happen if her mother and Sister Ignatius compared notes? Her heart began to thump with terror. If only she could prove it had happened, if only she could know whether it had happened or not . . .

Once or twice, she had with astonishment observed other people telling lies, besides herself and Eileen O'Brien – Eileen O'Brien could never know, when she looked with blank terrified eyes at the cane and howled the lie that nobody ever believed, how Isobel felt for her, howled with her inwardly – but Isobel was the only one who told lies without knowing it. Eileen O'Brien knew all right, when she shouted in despair.

Enough about Eileen O'Brien. Isobel might be standing in her place tomorrow. She couldn't face that thought for more than a sickening second. When she closed her eyes, she could see the nun, as tall as a tower, leaning forward, pale with anger, but that was no help – not to a born liar. 'A born liar, that Isobel! That child is incapable of telling the truth!'

She did have a lying sort of voice. Even when she was telling the truth it sank to a guilty whisper or rose to a shriek of denial which everybody took as proof of guilt. But she hadn't known about the school money, hadn't thought how often she didn't bring it, so where had the idea come from? Somebody must have said 'school money'.

Suppose truth was a handful of sand that trickled through her fingers, suppose something of the sort had happened, she had had the truth of it for a moment, but hadn't been able to carry it home? That thought brought a tormenting little hope that she might somehow get it back: could she repeat the exact words? Could she swear the nun had said 'every second week' or was it perhaps 'more than half the time'? And if she knew all the words, could she get them in the right order? She could of course go on like this for ever and reach no certainty; it was useless and fatiguing work, but it passed the time.

Bed was Isobel's kingdom; it was always a comfort to arrive there at last, and tonight particularly, she burrowed and snuggled and with a sigh of pleasure slid behind the curtain of the dark into her private world.

•

Robert came running, gasping, opened the door of the caravan and stumbled in. Gerald was there, hearing Angelo rehearse his part in the new play. They looked up, startled.

Angelo said, 'What's the matter?' but Robert couldn't speak. The stammer had come back. Gerald got up. (Gerald, husband of Antonia, who was Angelo's elder sister. Gerald, not the world's greatest actor, but handsome, a good singer, brave, an excellent swordsman.) He put his arms round Robert, said, 'Come on, old fellow. It's all right. You're safe here. Come on, tell us about it.' One of his hands were coaxing, too, stroking Robert's hair. 'Come on, now.'

Gerald could always manage the stammer; at last Robert's voice came clear.

'Two of my father's men, two of the bodyguard. In the inn. I w . . . w . . . went to ask . . .'

'Take it steady, now.'

'I asked if I could put up our poster on the wall outside. I saw them, in the mirror behind the bar. They weren't in uniform, but I knew them. I know them all.'

'Did you run?'

'Oh no. You've taught me better than that. I even put up the poster.'

Gerald's arms tightened about him for a moment.

'Do you think they saw you?'

'I don't know. When I got to the corner I ran, and there wasn't anybody behind me.'

'Well, we mustn't panic. Perhaps they aren't looking for you. They might have business of their own here.'

Angelo said, 'He'd better not go on tonight, just the same. I'll play the pageboy and he can stay in the van.'

'They'd be bound to search the vans if they were looking for him. I think he'd be better off on the stage.'

'But they'd recognise him!'

'No, they wouldn't. There's the make-up, and besides, who's going to imagine that our brilliant juvenile is the poor idiot prince? They've tricked themselves, making out that he's an idiot.' He pulled Robert's ear softly, because of the word 'idiot'. 'That's when you were in disguise, isn't it, old fellow? When you were living with them.'

It wasn't going to be so easy. Robert said unhappily, 'I would stammer. I know I would, if I thought . . .'

'Oh, hell.' Gerald was dismayed. 'You never have. Not on the stage.'

'But if I thought they were there, watching me . . . I couldn't be sure.'

'Well, we'd better not risk it. What's to be done, then?'

•

Isobel didn't know. The story stopped running; she was lying in her narrow bed in the dark, confronted by a sobering thought: Robert and Angelo were lies. It was all lies: the travelling theatre, Gerald and Antonia, the Maestro and Uncle Max, the terrible castle, all lies.

She wasn't going to give it up, either. She was sure of that at once. There was no living without the moments.

After her triumph in Uncle Max's new play, Antonia in front of the mirror takes off her heavy shining necklace – the knock at the caravan door – the famous producer: 'My dear girl, till this night I thought the great Leonora was dead.' – 'I am her daughter, sir.' – 'Of course, I remember now that she had a daughter. You have inherited her talent and her beauty. And the play, the brilliant play!' He sinks into a chair, shaking his head in amazement. 'To think that I came here for a joke! To laugh at the little travelling theatre! You must come to my theatre in the city!'

. . . the moment worn almost threadbare: Gerald drawing his sword against the kidnappers – the clatter and hiss of the weapons, the shouting, the wild hearty noise growing fainter as Robert runs for escape to the caravan and locks the door behind him.

. . . the moment for going to sleep to: the campfire at night, Antonia in slacks and sweater singing old folk songs to Uncle Max's guitar, Gerald putting out his arm to bring Robert close to him, Robert snuggling up with his head on Gerald's shoulder. (There must be moments when Antonia snuggles up to Gerald, but those are too tedious to contemplate.)

They were lies but not ordinary lies about mission money and chocolate and so on; there was something about them that was like the Virgin Mary and Baby Jesus.

False idols. Now she was in real trouble; what had been an interesting mysterious phrase in the catechism had come close, and worse, was somehow inside the inner room, having crept in in disguise. Now she came to think of it, she never did talk to the Virgin Mary any more. Robert and Angelo had taken her place, which proved it: they were false idols all right. That was mortal sin and her worst yet – a real hellfire affair, if she didn't give it up.

But they were so lovely, her people, so kind and happy and dear.

Of course they were lovely – that was what made them idols.

She had always thought with friendly exasperation of the sinners who doomed themselves to eternal hellfire – what was the matter with them, couldn't they do a simple sum? – but now she had a new idea about sin and discovered that the sum was not so simple.

Well, she would have to pin her hopes on a deathbed repentance, which wasn't so simple either. First of all, she had to know exactly what the sin was, to find the right name for it, and that wasn't always easy, then add it to the list she was memorising – there was a moral check in this, because if the list got too long she would be bound to forget something and then she'd be done for; one moral sin was enough to bring on eternal hellfire. There was a gamble in it too, because she didn't know what dying would be like; it might put everything out of your head. Still, she saw the deathbed repentance as her particular way to salvation, a kind of term test; term tests were about the only thing she could rely on herself to shine at.

With all this thinking going on, it was no use trying to get back to Robert and Angelo tonight. Glaring into the dark, she indulged instead in hatred of her mother, thinking of the hideous times when she asked, 'Do you love me?' The sound of the question was almost as irritating as the need to answer, coming in a set pattern like the same word clicked out on a typewriter, over and over again.

'Do you love me?'

'Yes.'

'Do you love me?'

'Yes.'

'Do you love me?'

'Yes.'

'How much?'

'How much?'

'How much?'

'How much? Threepenn'orth?'

'Yes.'

'Sixpenn'orth?'

'Yes.'

'One whole shillingsworth? Say, "Mummy, I love you one whole shillingsworth".'

'Mummy, I love you one whole shillingsworth.'

And if I'm such a born liar, thought Isobel, why does she believe me?

That spurt of malice brought relief, a dribble of tears and then sleep.

She wasn't sent to school the next day or the next, and after that she was sent to a convent in the next suburb. To reach it she had to climb through a fence and cross the railway tracks, a slight thing compared with the dangers that Gerald faced every day, but she hated it and slunk across, constantly bewaring of trains. However, the new school turned out to be a safe place, positively restful, and after a while she began to find it satisfactory that all the dangers of the day should be concentrated in one situation and overcome at once. After school she had time to walk the long way round, so every morning she used to scramble up the bank on the other side of the tracks with a feeling of relief that courage would not be required again that day.

One Sunday after Mass the parish priest came up to Mrs

Callaghan smiling and took her aside for a private talk. She walked home silent and blushing with satisfied pride, and next day she sent Isobel back to the local convent. She was not reluctant to go; by this time, she could rely on the scanty cover that time provides and she was curious to see Sister Ignatius again. Nothing had changed; she still spent her nights with Robert and Angelo, Gerald and the rest, she still accepted herself as a born liar, but she wanted to be a knowing sinner, to know the difference between truth and lies, and she hoped to find some clue in the nun's face, but Sister Ignatius didn't seem to notice her at all, so that hope came to nothing.

One day, she set out with her mother and her sister, all three dressed in their best, to visit Aunt Vera and the well-to-do cousins. On the way to the bus, Margaret said, 'I wonder whatever became of my gold chain bracelet?' She said this rather carelessly, in a tone of grown-up politeness; obviously the question had been on her mind for some time and she had not known how to ask it.

'Why, don't you remember?' Her mother spoke in a calm, far-away tone. 'Isobel put it on and went out for a walk and lost it. Wasn't it a shame?'

Isobel was about to shriek in her lying voice, 'I didn't, I didn't,' but she stopped herself in time. It was important not to break the silence.

She remembered something: Auntie Ann was saying to her mother, 'What's become of your diamond, May?' and her mother with a modest, worldly look was answering, 'Ssh! My solicitor,' following the words with a strange, shamefaced smile. Whoever this solicitor was, Isobel thought, he had the bracelet, too.

She pictured herself walking along this street with her arm dangling and the bracelet, much too big for her, slipping over her wrist and falling without noise. She saw this and she didn't believe it for a moment.

It was the silence. All the shouting, wailing, screaming of threat and blame that would follow the incident took place in the underwater world of the dream, where the swords hissed and clattered and the shouts rang out without disturbing the outer silence. This was even like a real dream, where extraordinary things happen and nobody shows any fear or anger. Margaret walked on in silence, frowning at the ground.

Isobel did not speak. It was a moment for breathing quietly, in relief. Sister Ignatius would never haunt her again. She knew she had seen a fireball, too. She could never be mistaken about that.

3 · The Grace of God and the Hand-Me-Down

The grace of God descended on Isobel during late Mass, one hot summer Sunday, and from the beginning she had a guilty feeling that it had come to her by mistake. Perhaps it was her neighbour who was in a perfect trance of prayer, and the gift was meant for her.

Isobel herself was conscious of the heat, of dust swimming in a ray of sunlight, of a patch of rosy light from a stained-glass window that was as ugly as a bag of jujubes but cast charming coloured shadows, of the open doorway drowned in the foliage of a peppercorn tree, but she had hardly been conscious of the service at all, until the sermon began.

That day it was given by a visiting priest, a young man with a gentle, easy voice and a matter-of-fact manner. 'Consider, my dear brethren,' he said sadly but without indignation, 'the sinful human soul. It is not beautiful. There are thick cobwebs looped in dirty corners, and scuttling insects which, only half-heartedly, we try to drive out.' This talk of scuttling insects struck home to Isobel, so she began to listen carefully. 'The one little window is so thick with grime we hardly see the sky. But if the light of the Holy Spirit should penetrate all at once into this cracked, cobwebbed cell, dear brethren, what a glorious change!'

These words had an effect on her more magical than moral. Her soul was bathed in a calm, delightful sunlight which remained through the rest of the Mass and when Mass was over she was sorry, for now she had to take her new treasure out into the uncertain world. She walked home behind her mother and Margaret, considering how to preserve it.

It wouldn't be easy. She could give up fighting with Margaret – she couldn't imagine now why she ever had. And stop being lazy, too. And answering back. That would be the hardest thing, but she could do it. Only. They were a kind of club, the virtuous, and they didn't like being asked to move up one.

The parish priest had come up to Mrs Callaghan after Mass one Sunday and said, 'You must be pleased with Isobel's exam results, Mrs Callaghan. A good, well-behaved girl besides, so the sisters tell me. And Margaret, too. You should be proud of your daughters.'

Mrs Callaghan had walked home almost silent, crippled by this injustice. At last she had drawn a deep breath and muttered, 'Oh, I could tell him a thing or two. Street angel, home devil. Street angel, home devil, that's Miss Isobel.'

But surely, thought Isobel now, you're allowed to be good, if you want to be? And looking at it another way, the harder it was, the better. You would know then that you deserved the light.

As soon as she got home, she took off her Sunday dress, hung it up, put on an old one and went into the kitchen to peel the vegetables and set the table for dinner. Margaret came in as she was putting the potatoes into a basin of cold water.

'It just so happens that it's your turn to wash up. You're not going to get out of it that way, coming in here and taking the easy job.'

First test. Isobel was careful.

'I forgot.' True. 'But I'll wash up, don't worry.' Offensive enough to be inoffensive.

'So you say.'

Mrs Callaghan had come in behind them.

'What's the matter?'

'It's her turn to wash up and now she's done the vegetables and set the table. I was just coming to do it.'

'I'll wash up. I just forgot.'

Her mother looked at her with a considering frown and said nothing.

During the meal she said, airily, 'It's too hot for you to go round to Auntie Ann's this afternoon, Margaret. Isobel will have to go.'

Margaret looked delicate, gratified, but faintly astonished.

There was a silence. They waited for Isobel to scream, I won't! I won't! It's not fair! I won't go!

Isobel said nothing. Dreamily, she chewed cold mutton and looked with wonder at past rages. How could it matter whether or not she went to Auntie Ann's? She liked going there. There was a shelf of children's books in the old dresser on the back verandah which was her delight and Auntie Ann would give her a glass of homemade lemonade.

Her mother said, 'What's come over you? You look like a cow chewing its cud.'

Margaret giggled. 'Perhaps she's been converted. Saint Isobel of Plummer Street.'

Knowing what to say was the hard thing. Isobel paused over it, then said simply, 'I don't mind.'

She knew as she said the words that they were inadequate but she realised too – it was a new idea – that there was nothing her mother could do about that. She would have to make do with them.

After a moment, her mother came to the same conclusion. With a harsh expulsion of breath in the tempo of laughter, she set about a boiled potato and said no more.

Isobel found her great-aunt dozing on a chair where the latticed roof of the fernery made a patch of shade and dank staghorns and hanging baskets of maidenhair suggested the idea of coolness.

'Trying to catch a breath of air, love. Fancy you walking round here in all this heat.'

'Mum sent me round with the meat press. She thought you'd be wanting it.'

'Well, that was nice of her. Put it on the kitchen table, my petty, and save my old legs.'

'Can I stay and look at the books?'

'Of course you can. There's a jug of lemonade in the ice-chest. Get yourself a glass of that but don't go drinking it while you're hot.'

Such warnings were the common coin of love to Auntie Ann. Isobel found them silly but soothing and liked being told not to sit on stone or drink water after eating grapes or sleep with the moon shining on her face.

She sat on the back verandah with a glass of lemonade beside her and a copy of *The Wide, Wide World* open in front of her. The book had large illuminated capitals at the beginning of each chapter and a coloured frontispiece of two girls wearing white pinafores and long black socks, with a frill of petticoat showing under their skirts.

Now for a lovely afternoon.

But it wasn't as lovely as usual. She was never again going to be happier in one place than another. Grace was like what the priest had said about Heaven, the eternal sunshine which had neither climate nor seasons nor night nor day. At the time she had thought, 'nice but dull' and the thought came again. But there was no going back; that was unthinkable.

She went home in time to set the table for tea, which they ate in most unusual quiet. When she got up to clear away, her mother said, 'That's enough, Miss Clever. Leave those dishes alone. Margaret doesn't mind doing her share.'

Margaret looked so taken aback that Isobel began to grin in triumph. In time she saw the danger: quietly and without warning, the world had nearly had her. Her temptation was to be not the rage of defeat but the smirk of victory, for practising humility she had acquired power. That was a new experience and dealing with it would be hard.

The next days passed quietly. The inward light stayed with Isobel, though all she had got from her attempt to gain merit was a material advantage. It was odd that, in spite of her reputation for laziness, she seemed to have less to do now that her mother watched to see that the chores went in strict rotation.

Over the tea table on Wednesday night, her mother said resolutely, 'I'm not going to put up with any more of this, Isobel. I want to know what you are sulking about.'

'I'm not sulking.' Astonishment brought the words out clear and strong, but she felt anxious. There was trouble coming.

'Don't give me any of your lies. What are you sulking about?'

'But I'm not. I'm not sulking about anything.'

Think of the inward light and hold on.

'Not sulking not sulking not sulking. You answer me. What are you sulking about?'

Oh, where was it, the tone of voice that made people believed (even sometimes when they were telling lies)? Isobel could never command it. She shook her head.

'Walking about looking down your nose too good to speak to anyone you nasty little beast. Miss Superior I can read you like a book. Telling me you're not sulking you brazen little liar. What are you sulking about?'

But it doesn't matter, as long as I'm telling the truth. If she doesn't believe me, that's her affair. This was so simple she wondered she hadn't thought of it before. There was another good thing about the state of grace: while that light continued to shine she knew she was telling the truth. Normally by this time she would have begun to think that she must be sulking and lying, since her mother was so sure about it.

There was a pause, so long that she thought it might be safe to pick up her knife and fork again, but as she stirred her mother said, 'I want you to tell me what you are sulking about, Isobel.'

She was really frightened now, wondering how long she would hold out, foreseeing the moment when she would begin to scream and scream.

She wasn't going to, not ever. She would think of grace and be still.

'Tell me.' Her mother's voice, which had been rising to a scream, turned calm and gracious again. Like somebody getting dressed. Isobel looked up and saw that her eyes were frantic bright. She doesn't want me to tell her, she wants me to scream. I do something for her when I scream.

Then she saw that her mother's anger was a live animal tormenting her, that she Isobel was an outlet that gave some relief and she was torturing her by withholding it.

Her father used to do that, sitting silently while her mother raged at him, chewing his food slowly, turning the pages of his newspaper deliberately – doing what Isobel was doing now. But one night he had put the paper down with a fierce thump and shown a white face, wild eyes and a mouth gaping as if his tongue was swollen. His chair had crashed over, he had picked up the knife from the bread board and run at her mother, who was cringing away with her head at a strange angle and a meek frown on her face, her hands out in front of her and the line of blood suddenly across her fingers.

But before that, when he had got up, before she saw

how real the knife was and how near, there had been two little glittering points of satisfaction in her mother's eyes, two little sea-monsters swimming up from . . . Standing there, the two of them looking at that awful astonishing blood, frightened like two children who had climbed too high in a tree and didn't know how to get down.

Peace in the house for a long time after that, a shamed, daunted peace.

But I'm not doing it on purpose to torment her, thought Isobel, so that's all right. She didn't care about her mother's suffering. Grace was selfish.

She said, 'I'm not sulking,' and this time the tone was right.

'Oh, you . . . you . . . you . . .', her mother said and stood glaring, words deadlocked in her throat. She pushed back her chair, left her dinner and went into her bedroom.

Silently, the girls finished their meal and cleared away, trying not to hear the strange yawning noises from the bedroom. At one moment Margaret drew breath and looked at Isobel reproachfully but whatever she had had to say died in her mouth.

Margaret came home late from school one day, looking tired and dizzy with delight.

'Where have you been?'

'We're doing a play at school. Twelfth Night. I've got a part. Olivia. Miss Ferguson says, is it all right to stay back and practise after school Tuesdays and Thursdays?'

She looked with sudden fear at her mother's frown.

'Miss Ferguson says it will give us a much better appreciation of Shakespeare.'

Margaret often began sentences with 'Miss Ferguson says . . .' Miss Ferguson was young and slender. She wore her fair hair cut very short and spoke calmly and boldly even to the headmistress, Miss Blundell.

'Well . . .' Mrs Callaghan shrugged. 'I suppose so. Just see that you're home at a decent hour, that's all.'

Margaret's face relaxed.

Why, Margaret's beautiful, thought Isobel.

It was an opportunity for grace, not minding that. She had to tell herself so, quickly.

There were real boys in the play, from the Boys' High School. Miss Ferguson the miracle-worker had talked Miss Blundell into it. Miss Blundell had called the cast together, told them what standard of behaviour was expected of young ladies and what confidence was being placed in them. Jessica Long, who was going to play Viola, performed Miss Blundell's speech for her friends in the playground, pulling her face into a delicious dewlapped solemnity, and Isobel was one of the crowd who gathered to watch, so she heard about the boys, though Margaret didn't mention them.

Isobel saw the seven exotic creatures (troubling in face, strangely satisfying in shape) crossing the playground, looking resolutely casual, on Tuesday afternoon.

Margaret came home at half-past five, tired, full of private joy, and sank into a chair.

Grace was wearing thin for Isobel. She had to do something quickly to affirm it. She shut her book, got up and began to set the table.

Since the scene at the tea table, her mother had spoken to her as little as possible, instead darting looks of luminous hatred at her – real hatred, no mistake about it. She needed armour against them, but then, she had it, not shining on the outside, but so long as she had the light inside, she was safe.

Now her mother said, 'You leave that alone. It's Margaret's turn.'

Margaret got up unwillingly and Isobel sat down, with grace still endangered. She could make a gesture, like saying, 'How did the rehearsal go?' but Margaret might think she was playing on their mother's annoyance. So she would be playing on it. She was jealous, and jealousy was no insect. She had better be quiet and concentrate on grace.

Margaret went to bed early. When Isobel came in, she found her propped against pillows, studying her part, her face peaceful and intent as she murmured, 'By mine honour, half drunk. – What is he at the gate, cousin?'

Shakespeare belonged to Isobel. It was hard to bear the sight of Margaret, so beautiful, and taking his words to herself. Grace, grace.

She got into bed in silence, thinking, 'I should offer to hear her,' but knowing that would be asking too much of herself.

Margaret said, 'Isobel?'

'Yes?'

'Don't tell Mum about the boys, will you? I mean, there's nothing wrong with it. It's all right, but, you know . . .'

Isobel was too astonished now to be jealous. Margaret was speaking to her in an ordinary voice as if she was a friend. Trusting her not to tell, too.

'No, I won't tell.'

'Oh, thanks.' She murmured, 'A gentleman! What gentleman?'

Things could change. That was the breathtaking thought.

Thinking Shakespeare belonged to her – that was an insect, all right. Shakespeare belonged to everybody, like God.

The play was a good thing, like a window opening, or at least air coming in from somewhere. Mrs Callaghan resented it, muttering as Margaret learned her part, 'You ought to be doing your homework instead of wasting your time on that . . .' She wanted to say 'rubbish' but was daunted.

'But Miss Ferguson says this is real study, just as important as homework.'

Isobel was beginning to feel sympathetic, anxious because Margaret did not scent danger.

Margaret came home one evening later than usual, as the immoral dark was beginning to fall.

'Where have you been till this hour?'

'Play practice.' Her eyes and her tone were remote. 'There's just this one scene we simply can't get right. Miss Ferguson had us going over and over it.'

'She's got no right, keeping you out till this hour. I've got a good mind to ring her up and complain.'

Margaret looked alarmed. 'She said we could go if we had to get home. I didn't think that it mattered.'

'You didn't think. You never do think. You see that you're home here at a decent hour or there'll be no more play.'

Margaret said sharply, 'I couldn't be expected to let them down now. You said it would be all right. If it wasn't you should have said so in the first place.'

Mrs Callaghan looked as if she had walked into a wall. She didn't recover in time to answer.

Next rehearsal day Margaret was late, but not as late as last time. Mrs Callaghan was waiting, so tense that Isobel got nervous and began to set the table because she couldn't sit still and was more nervous still when that brought no comment. When Margaret came in, her mother took a small brown-paper bag from the shelf beside the clock. Margaret turned pale at the sight of it and stood silent as her mother emptied the contents onto the table: a small sample box of face powder, a little tube of vanishing cream, a tiny sample lipstick and two pots of colour.

'What is this?'

'It's just some makeup, for the play.'

'For the play. For the play. You are chasing boys. Coming home at all hours hanging about God knows where. Chasing boys. That's why you're painting yourself up, I know. If it's for the play, why have you got it hidden, I'd like to know? Wrapped in your underclothes. For the play!'

Margaret shouted, 'I will not have you going through my belongings. I have one drawer to keep my things in and that is little enough. That drawer is mine and you will leave it alone. Please.'

Her voice was thin, her anger was forced and fragile – Isobel thought of the butterflies whose outstretched wings make an angry mask to frighten off the predator – yet it worked.

Mrs Callaghan cowered, white-faced and speechless, then burst into moaning lamentation: 'Who'd have children? Heartless and ungrateful. Give up everything you've got for your children and what do you get? Abuse. Speaking like that to your widowed mother. What will it be next? Cigarettes, I suppose, and god knows what else.'

Her voice throbbed with tragedy. She sounded very funny, and Isobel laughed.

She came to herself in dismay, startled by her mother's true suffering look. No more grace then. She sat appalled, still as a mouse, making a frantic act of contrition and waiting for pain to start. It did not start. Darkness did not set in. She had got half-way through the silent meal before she could accept that the light would go on shining.

A narrow escape, though, and she wished she knew why she had been spared. If only there were rules to keep, to be safe. It was the moment to pray for guidance, but she didn't want to bring her case to the attention of Head Office, which might decide to correct the original mistake. If God made mistakes, he certainly wouldn't want to hear about them. But the saints were different. She wished there was a saint in charge of grace, the way Saint Anthony was in charge of lost property. Somebody to pray to, to give her some help.

So began her study of the saints, on Saturday afternoons in the Public Library. *Lives of the Saints, The Oxford Dictionary of Saints* . . . she found out at once that grace was every saint's business, and they had some very funny ways of keeping it, wearing hairshirts, sitting on pillars – anyone who needed to wear a hairshirt, she thought, had a pretty easy life to begin with. She didn't want to be like them – she got a fright at Saint Augustine's cry in the garden, 'Not yet!' To think that one could have everything – love, talent, friendship, what he called 'the warmth of kindred studies', a taste for the theatre – and have to give it all up. Moral, stay out of the gardens. Still, she went on reading, fascinated by these holy men and women because, ratbag or martyr or angel of mercy, they had the world beaten, they were sure of themselves and made short work of parents and even of children. (How could Perpetua leave her baby? But she could, and that gave Isobel a glimpse of a splendid freedom in having no choice.)

As for keeping the state of grace, there was one message that came through, always: give up, sacrifice. 'Having sold all her goods to feed the poor . . .' 'He distributed his great fortune among the poor of the city . . .' Isobel had a few possessions to which she was attached, books, an enamel brooch and a china dog, but who would want them? They wouldn't go far in feeding the poor, either.

Then the funny side of it struck her and she began to grin. Thinking about feeding the poor, indeed – she was 'the poor'.

Meanwhile, the play was losing its glamour and becoming a trial and a burden like ordinary life. Margaret whispered her lines with a worried look, trying different intonations. It had become 'Scenes from *Twelfth Night*' and they had given up the idea of public performance. It was put on one afternoon at the Girls' High School and one afternoon at the Boys'. Margaret, in a borrowed long green dress looked pretty but was a stick, and so was Jessica Long, so brilliant an actress in the playground. Malvolio and Sir Andrew Aguecheek carried the day, but altogether, they were lucky to escape without disgrace.

It was impossible to tell whether Margaret was glad or sorry that it was over. Her feelings were no longer to be read. She had a new friend, Louise, and spent Saturdays at her house; the alliance with her mother had gone for ever.

Isobel was left to witness her mother's sufferings, which were real and ludicrous. She walked about white-faced, repeating, 'Who'd be a mother? Who'd be a mother? You do everything for them, you give up everything for them and what do you get for it? Forgotten as soon as it suits them, they're gone without a thought. Heartless ungrateful children.'

She spoke not to Isobel, but in her hearing, wanting her perhaps to repeat the lament to Margaret, or inviting her to a new alliance. Isobel kept her mind averted, but thought it was strange, as she speeded up her polishing of the kitchen floor, that she should be hurrying through the chores in order to desert this misery and go and read about saintliness and brotherly love. She could not help it; grace told her to withdraw and she did what grace demanded, though it was more of a holding position now than an inner joy.

'Is that all right? Can I go now?'

'Oh, if you call that polished. Do what you like. Selfish. You're all tarred with the same brush.' She was too listless for anger.

The girls happened to arrive home together one afternoon to find Aunt Noelene's car parked outside. They brightened. Though Aunt Noelene was an awkward, shaming character, her visit meant a present of ten shillings and her cast-off clothes, which were better than other people's new ones.

Mr Callaghan's two sisters had done well in the world – an injustice which annoyed Mrs Callaghan so much that Isobel used to tell the children at the convent stories about a will suppressed or even forged to cheat her father of his inheritance, but she had come to understand at last that her mother was angry with fate, as usual. Aunt Yvonne had married a property owner and lived in the country, as far away as Heaven. Aunt Noelene was the manageress of a dress factory and owned shares, had a car, took smart holidays and wore clothes that filled Mrs Callaghan with contemptuous pity.

'Poor Noelene. If she knew what a fool she looked in that get-up.'

The two women were sitting at the kitchen table, Mrs Callaghan calm and social, looking cheerful for the first time since Margaret's desertion, sipping tea from one of the good cups and making a tasty meal of Aunt Noelene in mauve crepe de Chine with two sleek russet foxes round her shoulders, each biting the other's thigh, their tails swinging free. The shaming thing about Aunt Noelene was that, though she was quite ugly, she dressed as if she was beautiful. Isobel didn't see why she shouldn't – why should the beauties have all the mauve crepe de Chine? – but Aunt Noelene, having let her dreams show, lacked the nerve to defend them. Under Mrs Callaghan's amused eye she cowered, burning with helpless rage, and even the foxes looked troubled.

Her voice too was harsh and sullen. 'Well, how are you two getting on at school?'

'They are both doing very well, thank you. Would you like another cup of tea?'

There was a bulky brown-paper parcel propped on a chair.

'No thanks, May.' Aunt Noelene made an effort. 'Isn't

Margaret shooting up? Getting more like Yvonne, isn't she?'

Mrs Callaghan dimmed a little at the mention of Yvonne. 'How is Yvonne? I haven't seen her since Rob's funeral.'

'I was up there for a week at Easter. They're all very well. Keith is helping Tom with the property full-time now, he wasn't interested in going to University. Hugh wants to do Law, he's the one with the brains. It's lucky one of them wants to go on the land.'

'It must be very nice, having a holiday in the country. I know poor Rob would have enjoyed it if he had had the chance.'

Disaster was coming. Margaret gave an anxious look at the parcel and Isobel shared her feeling. There was the ten shillings too.

Aunt Noelene stared at the table.

'When the doctor said that a change of air might work wonders, I wrote to her. Her only brother dying and she sent me five pounds. Towards a holiday. Five pounds.'

Aunt Noelene muttered, 'So I suppose you sent it back.'

Looking quietly contemptuous, Mrs Callaghan poured herself another cup of tea, steadily.

Well, there went ten shillings. She was going to regret it as much as the girls, but they both knew she couldn't give up her present enjoyment for its sake.

'For God's sake, May, why do you keep going over and over it? We've heard it all before. It's over and done with. Forget it.'

'There are things you'd like forgotten, too, I suppose. Like not going to visit your only brother when he was dying in hospital.'

'If I'd been allowed to know how sick he was . . .' Aunt Noelene was shouting now.

'Allowed to know. Didn't want to know. You and Yvonne have never wanted to know anything that didn't suit you.'

'Perhaps you've forgotten a thing or two, too. You haven't always been an angel.'

Mrs Callaghan breathed deeply. 'I want to know what you mean by that.'

Silence.

'Well?'

Aunt Noelene could not answer. Shakily, she searched in her handbag, got out two ten-shilling notes and put them on the table.

'For the girls.'

The girls held their breath. Was she going to say, 'Take your money!'?

No. Aunt Noelene had gone, the money was on the table, the parcel still on the chair.

Their mother sat staring into space. They did not dare to mention the parcel yet.

At last, since she didn't stir, Margaret said, 'Can we look at the clothes?'

'Do what you like.'

They opened it quietly, subduing enthusiasm. A navy skirt, a white silk blouse, a red jumper, a yellow dress . . .

It was made of buttercup-yellow linen, the yoke and the sleeves embroidered in white cutwork to a heavy lace.

Margaret said 'Oh!' and held it up. Pinned to the skirt was a sheet of paper with ISOBEL printed in large letters. Margaret said 'Oh!' in a different tone. Mrs Callaghan uttered a scream of anger, as if Aunt Noelene had left her an insulting message.

Isobel knew at once what she had to do: give up, sacrifice. It was harder than she had foreseen.

'You can have it if you like.'

She was glad that the words were out and couldn't be taken back.

'Do you mean it? Really?'

'Yes. You can have it.' Don't make me say it again.

'Oh, no,' said their mother softly. 'No. It's Isobel's dress and she's going to wear it.' She got up, saying to herself, 'That creature! That creature!' and walked out, holding her hands to her head.

The girls looked at each other, puzzled.

'You did mean it, didn't you?'

'Yes. Go on, try it on.'

Isobel was sure now. The state of grace, the peace and security of it, meant more than any dress.

She followed Margaret into the bedroom and helped her into the dress.

'It looks lovely.' So it did, and she didn't mind at all.

'Oh, Isobel!' Margaret hugged her briefly.

'Take that dress off, Margaret,' said their mother from the doorway. 'It belongs to Isobel.'

'But Isobel said I could have it.'

Isobel said, 'Aunt Noelene will never know.'

Her mother gave her a look of hate as she walked towards Margaret, who did not know what was happening and stood like a good little girl having a dress fitted till she heard the dull snap of threads and the tearing noise. She cried out then as if she had been hit.

'Damn you,' screamed Isobel. 'Damn you, damn you, it was mine. It wasn't yours to tear. It was mine and I gave it to Margaret. Damn you!'

She saw the look of peace and relief on her mother's face as she walked away and she knew what she had done. The old sick closeness was back and she was the same old Isobel.

Margaret was sitting on her bed dressed in her slip, stroking the torn yoke and sobbing.

'It's only a dress,' said Isobel. She had lost more.

'Oh, you shut up. You didn't want it, anyhow.'

It wasn't only a dress. It was much more, and it was gone, and so was the state of grace.

At that moment, Isobel thought such things were not for either of them.

4 · Glassware and Other Breakable Items

In the kitchen, Aunt Yvonne and Aunt Noelene were talking about clothes for the funeral.

'Of course they have to wear black,' said Aunt Yvonne. 'At their mother's funeral! I don't know what you can be thinking of.'

'The money.' Aunt Noelene's voice was rougher, and always had a defiant note in it. 'I'm thinking about the money. They haven't got much, poor kids. I don't mind buying them clothes but I think black's a waste of money at their age.'

'At their mother's funeral!'

It was interesting that Aunt Yvonne had the finer sentiments, but Aunt Noelene was going to pay for the clothes.

Isobel was packing most of her books into a box to be stored at Aunt Noelene's, and was feeling her first chill of sorrow at being parted from them. She hoped Aunt Yvonne would win the argument, for it was reassuring that grief had its uniform and its routine – she could join the army and become anonymous.

'All right. Have it your way. I'll take them into

Graces' this afternoon. And a pair of shoes for Isobel. I've never seen . . .' her voice dwindled and was lost.

Aunt Yvonne answered, 'They're lucky to have had a good education.'

Dead, thought Isobel, trying the word again. It still meant only silenced. There was no hope of calling up any decent feeling from her evil heart, which was rejoicing in the prospect of freedom and even of new shoes. She picked up Shakespeare, Byron, Keats and Shelley and carried them into the bedroom, where Margaret was sitting on her bed, dazed and weeping, silently and slowly, tears dripping like blood from a cut finger.

'Do you mind if I take the Shakespeare? It isn't mine but I'd like to have it.'

Margaret shook her head, sending two tears running quickly down her cheeks. It wouldn't do to tell her to cheer up. Somebody should be giving Isobel the opposite advice.

Yet there was in her, deeper than her relief, a paralysing sorrow, not at her mother's death but at being unable to grieve at it. That one was going to stay with her; she looked for distraction from it in the cheerful business of packing and buying new shoes, but knew that any cheerfulness was, in the situation, shocking. She feared she had shocked Aunt Yvonne already.

Perhaps the funeral would touch her feeling and make her a member of the human race.

'I heard Aunt Yvonne talking to Aunt Noelene in the kitchen. I think we're going to buy dresses for the funeral this afternoon.'

At that, Margaret began to sob, lay down and hugged the pillow to her face, crying, 'Poor Mum. Poor Mum.'

Oh, why couldn't she do that?

It was no better at the funeral. All that Isobel could think, of the coffin and the candles, the hymns and the praise, the relatives who never visited while her mother was alive, but came now with serious faces to the church and the grave, was that her mother had become like other people at last.

As they lowered the coffin into the ground, she told herself urgently, 'Feel something, feel something!' for this was her last chance, but she could only see her joy flaring like a great red flower among the pallid chrysanthemums.

Ritual had failed her. That depressed her so much that she became respectable and, in the car on the way back to the house, earned a kind glance from Aunt Yvonne, who looked up from comforting Margaret to see her dejected air and to misinterpret it.

'Now,' said Aunt Yvonne, as they sat drinking a cup of tea in the kitchen, 'we have to think what's to be done. I'd like to take the girls back with me for a while, to have a holiday and get over the shock.'

'I've got the chance of a job,' said Isobel quickly. 'I have to go for an interview tomorrow.'

Aunt Noelene said, 'But you haven't started at Tech.'

'They'll take me without shorthand and typing because I got honours in German. They want somebody to translate the German mail.'

'Well,' Aunt Yvonne uttered an inscrutable sigh, 'perhaps that would be the best thing.'

'Make sure you get your shorthand and typing,' said Aunt Noelene, frowning.

'Where is she going to live?' asked Aunt Yvonne, looking steadily at Aunt Noelene.

Isobel held her breath, but Aunt Noelene preserved a beneficent silence.

'I can get board somewhere.'

'Well, yes.' Aunt Yvonne rubbed her temples, wearily. 'I'll see to that before we go. And then there's the furniture.'

'What about Margaret's job?' Aunt Noelene sounded aggressive.

'It's not much of a job, is it? I don't see that it matters if she does give it up. She can do better than that.'

'If you think so.' They understood now that Margaret would not come back. 'The girls can pick out any bits of furniture they want to keep and I'll store them at home. We can get a dealer in to take the rest and be done with it.'

Isobel wept her first tears and wiped them away in surprise. She thought hard for something to ask for, to keep, but, except for her books, which hardly counted, she could find nothing. That dried her tears and deepened her depression.

Aunt Yvonne said, 'I might as well look through the sheets and towels and the crockery.' She sounded astonishingly refreshed by the thought. 'They're things you can always use.'

The girls were shamed, not by Aunt Yvonne, but by the poverty she was about to uncover. Aunt Noelene looked with quick deep contempt at Aunt Yvonne; Isobel caught the look and stored it away, as she did everything that reached her from the world outside.

Margaret and Aunt Yvonne sat together on the back seat of the taxi, as like as mother and daughter. It was agreed now that Margaret would make her home with Aunt Yvonne; she wore the dreaming look of one who has just received a declaration of love. Isobel sat beside the driver.

They were on their way to the boarding house the aunts had found for her, a respectable establishment where she would find young company, then to the railway station where Aunt Yvonne and Margaret would begin their journey home.

'Number a hundred and five,' said Aunt Yvonne to the driver. He slowed down while they peered at house numbers, Isobel breathing quickly in excitement. 'Here we are.'

The taxi stopped in front of a large two-storeyed house

of red brick with bay windows which glared at a small ragged lawn.

She got out. The driver got her case from the boot and set it beside her on the pavement.

'Well,' said Aunt Yvonne.

There was a moment of blankness. Something was expected; neither girl knew what it was. They looked awkwardly at each other. Aunt Yvonne looked disconcerted. Isobel had seen that expression on other faces. She had never been able to interpret it.

'Well,' said Aunt Yvonne very brightly, 'don't forget your board is paid till Sunday week. You have the receipt, haven't you?'

'Yes, Aunt Yvonne.' She added, 'Thank you,' though she thought it most likely that Aunt Noelene had paid her board. Still, the word filled a gap.

'Noelene will be in touch about the money for the furniture. Don't forget we expect you at Christmas.'

Isobel nodded.

Margaret leaned forward.

'Goodbye.'

'Goodbye.'

It wasn't a last word. It was a first word. She picked up her suitcase, walked to the front door and rang the bell.

Here we go.

The door was opened by a tall elderly woman, ruddy-faced and ginger-haired, who must be Mrs Bowers, the landlady.

'It's Isobel, is it?'

Time had carved a sourly humorous expression on her face and her voice matched it in harshness, but her words were welcoming.

'Come on in. We've been expecting you. Leave your case in the hall. I've just made a cup of tea. Your room's upstairs, first on the right with the door open. You'll find it all right, I don't take the stairs on account of my legs. Come and have a cup of tea before you go up.'

Isobel followed her along the hall into a large bright kitchen, where an old woman sat at the table slicing beans, or, it seemed, resting from slicing beans, while she stared with vague salt-water blue eyes into the distance. She was a real confection, the old woman, large and so soft she seemed to be made of whipped cream, and topped with a floss of silver hair.

'This is my friend, Mrs Prendergast. This is Isobel; she's taking Rosemary's room, you know. Lost her mother, poor little thing,' she added surprisingly.

Isobel was wearing her funeral clothes. Aunt Noelene had settled on a black skirt, which would be useful later, and a black blouse with white pin spots, in defiance of Aunt Yvonne. Isobel hadn't been quite aware till Mrs Bowers spoke that she was wearing mourning. She hadn't, after all, much choice.

Mrs Prendergast returned from the distance and focused her eyes. 'Sudden, was it? What was it? Her heart?'

Mrs Bowers said sharply, 'She wouldn't want to be talking about that. Now sit down. How do you like your tea?'

'No milk, thank you.'

From shyness her voice almost failed her, but this was acceptable in a poor orphan. She was able to drink her tea and eat a slice of cake in silence while the two women chatted.

'Thank you very much.' She set down her cup and stood up.

'Dinner's at half past six. The dining room's next door, through the hatch there. The bathroom's at the end of the passage upstairs. Change your linen Sunday morning. Madge will show you round. That's my daughter, Madge,' she added stoically.

Mrs Prendergast answered her tone, with sympathy.

'Still in with those people?'

Mrs Bowers shrugged. 'Doesn't do any harm, I suppose.'

Isobel wondered, as she carried her case upstairs, who the people were who caused concern in Mrs Prendergast and humorous resignation in Mrs Bowers. It appeared at least that Madge was flighty. What they called a mod, perhaps. Then she found the open door at the top of the stairs, went into her room and closed the door behind her. It was a commonplace little room but she was prepared to love everything in it: bed (slightly sagging), chair (straight), faded floral curtains at the window (her own window), combination wardrobe and dressing-table (lucky she didn't have many clothes), a grate in the corner, with a vase of paper flowers delivering the message that it was no longer used for fires, above it a shelf for her books. She unpacked them first: Keats, Shelley, Byron, Shakespeare, *The Last Chronicle of Barset*, from the library. She looked with regret at that. She had been reading the novels of Trollope and whenever she wasn't reading, no matter what was happening in the outside world, she was conscious of being in exile from Barsetshire. She resisted temptation and went on with her unpacking, having a modest ambition to meet life, to be adequate. She had an idea of a life of her own, like the room of her own, where she chose the furniture – no rages, no black passions, no buffeting from the world. She opened her suitcase and took out the box containing the new alarm clock, symbol of the new adequacy, wound it, set it down on the dressing table and began to laugh, because she did not know, not within an hour, what time it was, which marred the symbolic gesture or made it more symbolic still.

Putting her clothes away in a drawer she saw her face in the glass, so happy and hopeful that the likeness to her mother, which seemed to her usually to be a curse from birth, seemed unimportant. After all, a face was only . . . a glove? It didn't have to be clenched in rage. She couldn't like it: 'Sonnets from the Pekingese', she said to it, but good-naturedly. She observed it steadily, with detachment, and thought of changing her name to Maeve: Maeve Callaghan, poised, serene, quietly self-confident.

The dinner bell sounded and she went downstairs to meet the human race.

She had arrived first and stood back while they came in and took their places at the table: male, three – one old, two young; female, two – the younger must be Mrs Bowers' daughter, Madge, and to have thought her flighty! The word made Isobel fancy a monumental statue rising and flitting about on small delicate wings. The other must be called old, because her hair was grey, yet her face belonged to a heroine of romance, with delicate features, narrow blue eyes and full lips.

It was she who said, 'Hello. The new boarder. What's your name?'

She didn't, after all, say 'Maeve'. They would know. They would look at her with scorn and say, 'No, you're not. You're Isobel.'

'Isobel Callaghan.'

'She'll have Rosemary's place, I suppose, Madge.'

The statue nodded.

'Come and sit down, then.'

The vacant place was between her and Madge at the end of the table. The elderly gentleman (such a one as the words had been coined for) sat at the other end; he made a half-bow and gave a half-smile when the woman named him as Mr Watkin.

'I'm Betty, and that pair of larrikins are Tim and Norman.'

Tim was cheerful, pink-cheeked and blubber-lipped; Norman terracotta and hard-boned (she wondered what it would be like to touch him, then dismissed the thought with shame).

They had been talking about football as they came in, were carrying on the conversation at the dinner table and paused in it long enough to nod. If they were the young people who had made the house suitable for Isobel, they were quite unaware of their responsibilities.

'They improve on acquaintance,' said Betty, just as Maeve would have said it.

'I give you five to two they'll beat Souths,' Norman answered.

Meanwhile plates of soup began to appear in the hatch that opened from the kitchen, and Madge got up to bring them to the table. She was not, after all, monumental in size, but in stillness and dignity; she moved as if she were wearing an invisible robe and handed soup as if she were taking part in a religious ceremony.

During the main course, the young men's conversation turned from football to the charms of the new trainee at the Bank: figure (Norman sketched on the air, what words could not convey), face (not bad either, not bad at all), altogether a peach, a trimmer, a table bird, everything indeed that Isobel was not and, though she was determined on calm acceptance, the thought was saddening.

Betty looked up at last from her roast lamb and said with amusement, 'Don't tell us, tell her.'

Norman said, 'We're tossing up on that.'

'Be sure to let us know how it comes out. We'll be suffering the suspense with her.'

The remark was crushing and silenced Norman, yet he accepted it with a grin.

Was it dialogue? Were they acting in a play?

After roast lamb came tinned peaches and custard, all conveyed by Madge from the hatch, where she stacked the used plates.

After dinner, Betty said to Madge, who was clearing the table, 'I'll show Isobel around, if you want to get away.'

Madge's response was slight, a vestige of nod and smile, yet gave a glimpse of a private joy.

Norman was aggrieved. 'No cards tonight?'

'This won't take long. The boys are learning to play bridge,' she added to Isobel. 'Do you play cards?'

'No. I've never tried.'

She hoped nobody would ask her to try.

'Mr Watkin is the expert. He is very patient with us.'

'You are too modest, Betty.' Mr Watkin performed his courtly minimal bow. 'And the boys are coming along well.'

Betty answered with a smile (how beautiful!) as she led Isobel out of the room and upstairs.

'Let me see. Change sheets and towel on Sunday morning, take dirty linen to the laundry – black mark if you don't. I do my own room, to save Madge – Mrs B. doesn't do upstairs because of her legs.' Her tone reserved a judgment on Mrs Bowers' legs. 'Mop and dusters in this cupboard if you want them. Bathroom this way – if you want to use it in the morning be early and look sharp.'

'How early?'

'Before six-thirty. Breakfast at seven-fifteen, we're all off to work by eight. You too, I suppose.'

'Starting tomorrow.'

'Good. Now, the sins – don't sit in your room at night, Mrs B. watches the electricity bill like a hawk. Has she given you a door key? You'd better ask for one, doors locked at half past nine or when the other one goes home – that's any time after dinner. Ironing – that costs you, she keeps the iron under lock and key and it's two bob an hour or two bob a time – fair enough, of course, but save up an hour's worth. Likewise for washing – it's free but don't be forever in the laundry. Mind you, the food could be a lot worse. I think that's all. If I've forgotten anything, just ask. I'd better be getting downstairs. The old gentleman does look forward to his game.'

Left to her unpacking, dismissing with regret the dream of a reading light and a nightly haven, Isobel reflected that Betty hadn't told her the most important thing – how to be like her: cool, kind and self-possessed, able to accept the peculiar Madge, to deal easily with the boisterous young men (but that from a height of beauty and elegance Isobel could never attain). Still, such a manner must be for all seasons. The seasons of Maeve, who would study to attain it.

With the last piece of underwear folded in its drawer, she paused to consider right behaviour.

No, it wouldn't do to take Trollope down to the dining room, not the first night. Was she ever going to find out where Mr Crawley got the cheque?

Right behaviour first. She went downstairs to the dining room, to watch the bridge game.

The game absorbed the attention of the players. They looked up and nodded briefly when she came in, then went back to studying their cards, the boys with some pain. What a deadly serious game it was. When they had played the hand, Mr Watkin reconstructed it, analysed it and lectured the boys on their errors, but kindly and gravely.

Isobel almost yawned, which would not have been right behaviour. She could have brought Trollope, after all. Suddenly, the yawn came over her, a real one, of fatigue. She tried to bite it back, but ineffectually.

Betty looked up and smiled (beautiful!). 'Ready for bed? It's been a long day.'

Isobel nodded, still struggling like Laocoon in the grip of the yawn.

'We usually have a cup of tea about ten, if you feel like waiting for it.'

Laocoon managed a headshake.

'See you at breakfast then. A quarter past seven.'

The office of Lingard Brothers Importers was on the first floor of a narrow building in Pitt Street. At half past eight next morning, Maeve Callaghan stepped up the stairs, washed, combed and neatly dressed, opened the door marked Lingard Brothers Importers, and entered a small room where four desks bore four typewriters still under oilcloth covers. There was one young woman already there, standing beside the rear desk sorting papers.

'You're Miss Callaghan, are you? Mr Walter is in his office. This way.' Her tone was not quite hushed, yet was subdued by the importance of Mr Walter, who had seemed at the interview to be a worried, flurried little man. She tapped gently at his door, opened it and said, 'Do you have a moment, Mr Walter? It's Miss Callaghan, starting work today.'

Mr Walter was busy. 'Just a moment. Take a seat, Miss Callaghan. Thank you, Olive.'

He read to the end of the letter he was holding, set it down and looked up.

'Well, Miss Callaghan. Your duties. The German mail, of course. That's the most urgent matter. General duties, you'll be under Olive's authority for those, but the mail must come first, you understand.'

'Oh, yes.'

'Good. Good. Everything else can wait till the backlog is cleared away. Except perhaps the petty cash. You could handle the petty cash at the same time, I think.'

'I'm sure I could.'

'Good. It's quite a responsibility.' He reached for a black japanned box, set it on the folder of mail and slid them across to her.

'The receipt book is in the box. You must not issue cash

without getting a receipt and the key must not leave your possession. You make your balance every Friday morning and Mr Richard will check it. Any deficiency will be made up out of your week's salary.'

'Do I take anything that's over?'

Everything came to pieces.

She had meant it as a kind of grace, so that he could say, laughing, 'There's never anything left over,' and she could answer 'I hope there's never any deficiency either.'

Instead, there he was, staring and stumbling in real misery while she was left holding her unwanted joke.

'But if there was anything over . . . Mr Richard, you see . . . it would be an advance, probably, from Mr Richard . . . he might have forgotten . . .'

'It's not very likely to happen.' She knew that the rescuing tone would give offence too, but there was no help for it.

He pressed a bell. The gesture seemed to restore him a little. The sight of Olive, who came in answer to the bell, restored him further.

'You'll keep an eye on Miss Callaghan, will you, Olive? Look after her, show her the ropes. And remember, the German mail has priority.'

'Yes, Mr Walter.'

Something in Olive's tone suggested a discreet and sober uniform. She changed out of it when they went back to the small room, where now two girls were each uncovering a typewriter.

'Well, this is Isobel. Rita and Nell.'

Rita was a gypsy girl and flashed a gypsy smile, Nell, small, sandy and freckled, had a face like an agreeable little fist. Olive had a beautiful calm madonna face and a slender torso, but set on a solid rump and legs, as if someone had made a mistake in assembling two statues.

'This is your typewriter, dear. Paper and carbons in this drawer. Mr Walter likes one carbon.'

'But I can't type.'

Olive looked startled.

'I was told that would be all right, because I knew German.'

'Well, just do your best. Would you like me to put the paper in for you?'

'Yes, please.'

'Right. Carbon this way up, don't forget that. Shiny side towards you as you feed it in. The margin's all right. Make sure the paper is straight. There you are!'

Left alone, she looked askance at the strange machine and opened the folder. She spent a happy forty minutes then, meeting Mr Vorocic the manufacturer of glass in Czechoslovakia, feeling for the many mischances which had held up his shipments as well as raising his expenses – *a heavy burden for a man with responsibilities towards a numerous family* . . . (How many children? She fancied a family photograph with Mr Vorocic seated, dignified but anxious, collared, tied and suited, next to his small worried wife and, flanking them, the two youngest, a boy and a girl . . . sailor suits went out last century. Come on, get on with it.) A shipwreck on the Danube had (put paid to?) the consignment on which he had been depending to supply the order in question . . imagine, the Danube existed, and so, for that matter, did shipwreck, all of them tied together by the shining glassware set out on long tables in the big showroom which was the centre of the establishment.

The moment came. The typewriter must be faced. She stared at it hopelessly.

Well, that was a familiar feeling and she was used to dealing with it, in the school gym: the comic strut towards the dreadful parallel bars, the ironic bow with which to acknowledge ironic applause.

She turned and said loftily, 'Can anyone tell me how to extract a capital letter from this apparatus?'

It was the gypsy girl who came, laughing. 'Oh, you are a card! Here, press this down. Oh, wait a minute!' She wheeled paper and carbon out of the machine, went to fetch a sheet of waste paper and wheeled it in. 'Now watch. Space bar. Capital letter. And if you want one of these, press down the same as for capitals. Now: The quick brown fox jumped over the lazy dog. Have a go. Right. Now put your paper back in. See this thing, Forward to open, back to close . . . Now are you right?'

Dejected and awed by this display of competence, Isobel nodded and began with painful effort to transfer Mr Vorocic's anxieties to the page. She felt closer to Mr Vorocic than to anyone nearby.

In spite of her kindness, Rita giggled over the tentative pecking noise of the keys.

'I can't help it. You sound like a drip in a tap!'

Isobel retorted, 'Mind who you're calling a drip!'

'No offence meant, I'm sure.'

This was just like school, therefore endurable, but disappointing. She had hoped for an improvement. She had produced two-thirds of a page of typing, with great labour, when she sensed body warmth behind her and, in self-defence, assumed a sprightly touch on the keys.

'Can't you type any faster?'

The voice squeaked, so that she looked up expecting a mouse of a man but saw a bulky form, grey as cobwebs, a big sallow face with cheeks that sagged like buttocks under suffering dark eyes.

'Mr Richard,' Olive said quickly, 'Isobel has never used a typewriter before.'

'I'm just finding out where the letters are. They seem to be very oddly arranged.'

Behind her, a scandalised titter informed her that a typewriter was a religious object.

Mr Richard too seemed to find the remark offensive. He glared, sighed deeply and went sullenly away.

But why?

Sometimes she thought she carried an invisible knife, wounding people without being aware of it. The typewriter keys were really very oddly arranged.

Olive said, 'Don't worry, dear. Just do your best. And Mr Richard . . .' but she decided not to finish the sentence.

Mr Richard came back. She was finishing the first letter. He stood behind her, watching.

I'm not here. I'm in Czechoslovakia with Mr Vorocic. She wheeled the page out of the machine, put it with the first one. He took it without speaking and walked away. She turned to look at the other girls, but every head was bent, every face hidden.

'What did I do?' She wanted to shout that aloud but turned instead to the second letter of the pile. Halfway through it she paused. *Seile*. What were *Seile*? Whatever they were, they had *gelockert* themselves, with bad results.

'Is there a German dictionary in the house?'

'Why, no. Don't you have one?'

Dread drags me, dread drags me to drowning.

'No. I didn't think about it.'

Would they sack you the very first day? Not lunch time yet. She had offended two bosses, humiliated herself at the typewriter and failed in German. Olive's look gave her no comfort. She stared at the sentence as if it might unfold. 'Again a misfortune!' Mr Vorocic had cried. A misfortune which had led to some breaking of glass. Whatever it was, it had happened *wegen des Windes*. A treacherous stream, the Danube. Treacherous to Isobel, too. Where Mr Vorocic lamented, she felt inclined to whimper.

'It's only ten minutes to lunch,' said Olive. 'Couldn't you go out and get one?'

'I suppose I'd better.'

Aunt Noelene, who talked as calmly about money as if it was geography, had said, 'You'd better keep a pound or so, to tide you over the first fortnight. You'll need money for fares and lunches, you know. If anything else comes up, let me know.'

She considered her indebtedness to Aunt Noelene: the mourning clothes, a pair of shoes, two weeks' board and five pounds for extras. Out of that she had kept one pound five, of which she had still a pound and two shillings. One did right and it still wasn't enough. Lunches would have to go. She would go for a walk at lunch time so that nobody knew.

When the other girls stood up and stretched, away from the typewriters, ready for lunch, she got up too, and went out into the street, heading for Dymocks. She had walked one block and a half when she stopped, not hopefully, but out of habit, in front of the bargain basket at the door of a secondhand bookshop. Impossible to pass the two-shilling basket at the bookshop, whatever the circumstances. The red, black and gold took her eye, but did not convince her. Yes, it was. It was a Langenscheidt, a paperback Langenscheidt, battered and loose in its cover. She opened it, calm in a shock of relief. There was *Seile*: ropes. And now she remembered *locker*. *Locker* meant loose, didn't it? She took the book into the store. The proprietor looked at it with contempt and said, 'I won't charge you for that. You can have it.'

'Thank you.' Oh, thank you, blessed Mary.

Fine talk from an atheist, that was. Maeve hadn't lasted long, either.

The bookman's contempt (which was, after all, a cover for kindness) made the book more precious to her. She carried it as if it had virtue, like a talisman stone. Speaking of virtue, there was no doubt bad luck was a vice and poverty a fault of nature which must be concealed. One could bear that while good luck was possible.

The afternoon went better. The drip of the tap grew faster, German no longer alarmed. Mr Richard came back twice, once to collect a finished letter, once to sigh harshly over an unfinished one and wait while she typed the last lines.

I am not here, I am in Czechoslovakia.

At five o'clock, when they covered their typewriters and got ready to go home, Olive said to her, 'Isobel, try not to mind Mr Richard. He means no harm, you know.'

She must mean, that he meant harm but could do none.

'Of course I don't mind.' She put on a coy look. 'I had no idea I was so fascinating.'

Olive looked startled. 'Well, that's the way to take it,' she said, but doubtfully.

'You're a sketch, you are,' Rita said, and yawned. 'See you tomorrow, girls.'

Isobel put the German dictionary away in a drawer and gave it a secret affectionate pat. It shed its virtue over the memory of the day.

There was no reading that evening. She could hardly keep a decent countenance during dinner and went to bed straight after.

The next day was peaceful. Mr Richard was not there, and the German mail went faster. Only two letters left to translate.

Betty was not at dinner. The young men were subdued, which was odd, because it was Betty who subdued their excesses. They went out after dinner; Madge disappeared; only Mr Watkin was left in the dining room, doing a crossword puzzle in the daily paper. Isobel brought down her book and spent the evening happily in Barsetshire.

Next day she finished the German mail in the morning and spent the afternoon in the storeroom checking invoices while Frank, the storeman, unpacked glasses.

'Six etched Bohemian, stemmed. Azure. 0 dash 234. Six ditto lilac. 0 dash 235. Six ditto clear . . .'

Frank was a neat, cheerful little man who radiated some of the virtue of the chance-found German dictionary. He handled the pretty glasses with a secure and gentle touch and called Mr Richard the dickybird.

'You couldn't trust the dickybird with this job,' he said. 'He's a disaster.'

She had suspected he might be.

'He's a suffering soul, see, and he takes it out on the glasses. And then, when he breaks one he suffers worse, because it's money down the drain.'

'I wouldn't trust myself with it, either,' said Isobel, and went on quickly, 'Aren't you a suffering soul, then?'

'Some can wear it, some can't.'

He lifted a rose-tinted goblet out of the packing straw, wiped it briskly and delicately with a cloth and held it to the light.

'Pretty.'

'Not top quality. Pretty enough. Now, where's its number?'

Between the pretty glassware and the plain talk, the easy, sensible employment, that afternoon passed pleasantly and five o'clock came unlooked for.

Away from Plummer Street, at ease in her own large kitchen, Aunt Noelene made a new impression.

She sat at the kitchen table; sunlight through the window lit the brilliant silk shirt she wore over narrow black pants, but did not make her ridiculous; one did not think, of her keen bony face, whether or not it was plain. She was scribbling a sum on a notepad.

'So, when you've paid your board, you have twelve and six left for the week. You won't get far on that. I'll fix the Business College. I'll send them a cheque for the term.'

'But, Aunt Noelene, I don't need shorthand, and I can type well enough for the German mail.'

'With two fingers. You keep that up and you'll never learn to type properly. And suppose this job folds? Where would you be then? You take my advice and get your qualifications while you can.'

'You do too much for me. I don't want to be a burden.'

'Well, that's . . .' Aunt Noelene snapped the remark off cleanly but too late. Isobel was blushing as the past rose round her like a stench of stale urine. In a less boisterous tone Aunt Noelene went on, 'You can't be expected to look after yourself at your age. Who else is going to look out for you, for God's sake?'

She went back to her sums. 'You'll need to eat out, three nights a week. You'll be paying for meals that you're not getting, that's a nuisance. No use asking for special rates at a boarding house. You end up being a skivvy. What's it like? The boarding house?'

'Oh, good.'

'Glad to hear it.' Aunt Noelene was finding her heavy going. 'Three pounds a month ought to do it. Make it four, a bit over for a bit of fun. You can come here for lunch, the first Sunday in every month, and I'll give you four pounds to tide you over. Now, that means I'll expect you on the fifth. If something happens that you can't make it, ring me up. You have my number, don't you?'

'It's too much.'

'You might as well have it now as after I'm dead. It's now that you need it. Don't look so down. We'll cut it out as soon as you get your rise. You'll just have to see to it that you do get it.'

At the thought of asking Mr Walter for a rise, Isobel felt faint.

'Won't they give it to me, without my asking?'

'No.' She made a comic turn out of saying so, looking dead-eyed at Isobel and wagging her head. 'Understand this. You will get nothing out of this world unless you fight for it.'

Fate was stricter than any headmistress. She must fight for money or be a burden on Aunt Noelene. Both prospects were intolerable, but not equally. She thought she could learn to fight rather than impose on Aunt Noelene.

"You want to keep your eyes open at the office and find out what's what. What do you do, apart from the mail?'

'Keep the petty cash, check the invoices when Frank unpacks the glass. I help him to polish it and set it out in the showroom and sometimes I take the mail to the GPO. Otherwise I do anything Olive wants – filing, mostly.'

'In fact, you're the junior, except that you translate the German mail. For a junior's wages. They sound like shysters to me.' She frowned and rubbed her thumb across her chin as she reflected. 'You've started off on the wrong foot, there. It's a special skill, the German, and you should have a loading, but you'll see, once they've got it for nothing, they'll go on taking it for granted. Who did the job before you came?'

'I don't know. They never mention it.' She added with feeling, 'Perhaps she threw her typewriter at Mr Richard.'

Aunt Noelene's laugh must be what was called a guffaw. 'Mr Richard! What a berk! Lord of the Manor, is he?'

'There's Mr Richard and Mr Walter, you see.'

'Dick and Wally, right. This Olive is the head girl, I suppose?'

'Yes.'

'Who else is there? Who takes the dictation, does the shorthand for Wally and Dick?'

'Rita, mostly. Olive and Nell do sometimes, when Mr Stephen is in and wants something done. I've only seen him once. He's the salesman.'

'You'll have to find out a few things, like what pay the others get. And find out about the one whose place you took. Are you making friends with anyone?'

'Well, Frank, I suppose. That's the storeman.'

There was a pause, Aunt Noelene said, 'I need a drink. I could do with a gin and tonic. Can I get you something? Lemonade?'

'No. Thank you.'

Having fixed her drink in silence, and carried it back to the table, she said earnestly, 'Look, love, I don't think you'll make it. You're no fighter. They'll tread you into the ground.'

Isobel had not known life was like this. She had expected it to be simpler.

'Why don't you go for teaching? Your Leaving pass was good enough. Apply at the end of the year. You'd get an allowance, you can live here if you like, get your own meals. There's a room at the back, even got a sink and gas ring. I used to let it before the business took off, don't bother now. You'd be independent and you'd meet a few people of your own type, go to dances and such and have a bit of young life. Why not?'

'I didn't like school. I don't want to stay here all my life.'

'I can sympathise with that. OK. But there are other jobs. Librarian, what about that?'

Isobel sat silent and dejected.

'All right. Give it till the end of the year. From what you say about those people, I think if you want to get anywhere there you'll have to hold a gun at their heads. You have to be prepared to tell them you're leaving; if they let you go, we'll think about a change. How about it?' Her purse was on the dresser. She got out the four pounds Isobel didn't deserve and didn't know how to earn. 'This is for your first month. And try to put a bit away every month. Even if it's two bob in a money box, try to get a bit behind you. Well, I'm glad you can smile.'

'I was thinking about Mr Micawber. In David Copperfield. "Annual income twenty pounds, annual expenditure nineteen pounds, nineteen and six, happiness." '

'Well, yes,' her aunt said vaguely. 'That's the idea.'

Mr Micawber seemed to have been the last straw for her. She drank her gin in silence. They were both relieved when the phone rang in the hall.

Isobel thought she could hear relief in Aunt Noelene's voice as she said, 'Oh, Stan. That's OK.' Laughter. 'I'd have had a piece of you if you had been there. You and your certainties! . . . No, not too bad, made it up just about on Peter's Dream in the fifth . . . twenty to one . . . Vi and her magic pin again . . . Yes, I told her she'd better get a forked stick and take up water divining, she'd be a sensation.'

Aunt Noelene had tamed money, made it into a kind of playmate, a spirited horse, great fun if treated with caution.

'No, changed my mind at the last minute, fancied The Oracle both ways and it came in second.'

People spoke poetry. Aunt Noelene spoke poetry: Peter's Dream in the fifth, The Oracle both ways. So did the boys at the boarding house, with their football teams, their Eels and Tigers, their Saints and the rest, their dishes and peaches.

Why did this fill her with anguish, with longing and a sense of exile? Longing for what? Exile from where?

'Good. We'll get up a game then. Friday night, fine. I'd better go. Got my niece with me, Rob's girl, you know.'

Would it please if she spoke of her father? She did not know what to say that would please, she did not know how to please. She is doing all this for me because she is Aunt Noelene, not because I'm Isobel. More honour to her.

Yet Isobel could have wished to have something to give in return.

Things went better after lunch. They rummaged among Aunt Noelene's overflowing possessions and she came back to the boarding house with a red belt to brighten up the black outfit, a nearly new handbag, a half-knitted sweater and a winter coat of old-fashioned cut. Aunt Noelene had been doubtful about the coat: 'Had it for years. Kept it because of the fur. I meant to take the fur off but never got around to it.' The fur was a deep spreading collar, deep cuffs, and a narrow trim that outlined the two fronts and the wide flaring hem. 'I don't know. It's out of style but it doesn't look too bad. Maybe it's so far out it's in.' The alternative was to break into the furniture money to buy a coat. The furniture money was a cheque for twenty-two pounds, with which she was to start a bank account.

Isobel thought the fur-trimmed coat was beautiful and gained approval from Aunt Noelene for keeping the furniture money intact.

In spite of that, the general effect of the visit was depressing. Until Aunt Noelene had explained to her the frightening living nature of money, how it had to be hunted, seized and tamed, she had been satisfied with her progress. Everything was manageable except Mr Richard, who still came to loom behind her clucking and sighing.

'There are two ways of taking it,' Frank had said to her as they unpacked glass in the storeroom. 'There's inner calm, not worrying about him at all. But it's got to be genuine. If you're putting on an act, calm outside and boiling inside, that's no good. It takes too much out of you.'

'I thought, if I pretended not to care, he'd get tired of it and go away.'

'I wouldn't depend on that. Besides, I reckon he'd know. People like the dickybird, they don't know much but they've got their specialities. If you're putting on an act, he'll see through it. If you're boiling inside, you got to tackle him. Just say, quiet and polite, "I'm sorry I'm keeping you from your work, Mr Richard".'

His primmed mouth and dulcet tones had made her giggle with joy.

' "Could I bring it in to you as soon as it is finished." ' He added soberly, 'That's the trouble, you know. He hasn't got any work, poor dickybird. He hasn't got the brains for business and he hasn't got the hands for glass. I wouldn't have him in here for quids, mucking about with my glasses. It's Mr W. that has the brains and it's Mr S. that has the looks and style. That's no excuse for bullying you. I think you've got to tackle him, myself. Give yourself a bit more time to get settled in and then tell him, nice and polite, to get his lubberly great frame out of your living space.'

Isobel had giggled again but had decided silently on inner calm. When Mr Richard loomed behind her she could tell herself she had chosen to bear it. It made a change from telling herself she was in Czechoslovakia.

She was altogether satisfied with herself and brought her book down to the dining room after dinner, conscious that she had been adequate to the day. It wasn't easy to read in the dining room. The bridge players took the table, where the light was good, but she made herself a spot in the corner, out of their way, where it was still possible to read.

For all their talk about peaches, dishes and little bits of fluff waiting to be picked up, Tim and Norman seemed to live a life as restricted as her own. They were happy to sit at the table studying their bridge hands, embryo bank managers learning their social skills.

There were evenings when Betty didn't come home to dinner. She had a job on the management side in a big hotel in the city. 'Working back,' Mrs Bowers would say, with the raised eyebrows of one who didn't believe a word of it. On those nights the boys were as rowdy as poltergeists, switching a yelling wireless from station to station, playing a kind of football with a matchbox, shouting in frivolous arguments, practising Indian wrestling. Madge would disappear, always. Mr Watkin sat at the table transferring information from newspaper cuttings to a large hard bound ledger. Isobel would sit at the table too, but the improvement in the light did not compensate for the destruction of her peace. She would wonder that frivolity should seem so like misery.

At last Mrs Bowers would call out from the kitchen, 'What are you two doing in there? Knocking the house down?' or 'Not so much noise, please!'

Norman then would grow silent and sullen, shrug his shoulders and say to Tim, 'Coming down the street for a milkshake?' and Tim, with an exaggerated hangdog look, would follow him out.

One bridge night – she had come nearly to the end of *Framley Parsonage* and was bent intently over her book – she felt a light blow to her cheek, like an insect alighting, and put up her hand to trap a ball of paper.

Norman was looking at her with a fierce grin. 'It's alive! It breathes!'

She lifted her book as a shield and to hide the excitement which was making a fool of her face. Her heart was thudding, too. She held the book in front of her face until her heart settled and she could involve herself again in the troubles of Mark Robarts. As soon as the excitement had passed, she was ashamed that such a little notice should cause such a flurry.

Two nights later it happened again. This time she was

ready; she caught the ball of paper, cried with delight 'A love letter,' stroked it smooth and added with disappointment, 'It's in code.'

Norman said impudently, 'Why would I be sending you a love letter?'

'Why would you be sending me anything else?'

She was delighted to be invited to join the games young people played, and flattered herself she did it well. (Elegant and spirited: 'La, Sir!')

Betty said, 'I don't think it's a love letter.'

'Oh, well. I shan't decode it then.' She crumpled the paper again and returned to her book.

After that, she read in peace and some disappointment, for a week or two.

She was wriggling, trying to find a better position, holding her book to the light, when Norman called to her, 'Careful, Isobel! You'll ruin your eyes! Men never make passes at girls who wear glasses.'

'Seldom,' she amended. 'That's the line. Men seldom make passes at girls who wear glasses. And where did you learn that? Did someone recite it to you?'

She looked up and found his gaze fixed on her, tense and dull with hatred. The invisible knife again. This time, after the the first jolt, she was not sorry. If it was not a game but a battle, she was glad to fight it even though she wouldn't have had the nerve if she had known.

It was sad that the admired Betty was looking at her coldly and said, in a voice as cold as her look, 'It's your bid, Norman.'

She saw no sympathy anywhere, but surely she was entitled to read, had seen to it that she inconvenienced no-one. People who wanted her to give up reading were asking too much without offering anything in return. Right behaviour didn't work unless everyone practised it. Well, now she knew where she stood; there was comfort in that.

She was more at home in the kitchen. where she had the status of a domestic pet. On Saturday afternoons she was fed tea and cake and listened to the conversation of Mrs Bowers and Mrs Prendergast. Mrs Prendergast was an admirer of death, entranced by its ceremonies, awed by its sudden captures, marvelling at its rare defeats. Small coffins and large funerals, broken hearts and lovely wreaths travelled on the placid unchecked stream of her conversation. Mrs Bowers was the enemy of sex and marriage. Her attitude towards sex was simple: it was a disagreeable penalty imposed on the goodlooking; having served her own time, she grew peevish with plain girls who did not know their luck. While Mrs Prendergast reminisced, she turned the pages of papers and magazines looking out for a mention of the enemy, to read it aloud, saying to Isobel with discreet disgust, 'You're better out of that sort of thing.'

'Doesn't know what she's in for,' she would say, of poor brides, rich brides, scandalous brides who must surely know what they were in for, while Mrs Prendergast would be reminded of a funeral that forestalled a wedding, or one that followed close after.

Isobel thought of them as the Fates; she listened passively while she drank her tea.

Mrs Prendergast, though her subject was grisly, had a weird talent for anecdote.

'I had such a nasty dream about Fred Williams. It's left me all upset. Poor Fred!'

'Why, what's happened to Fred?'

'Well, nothing so far, I suppose. It was this dream I had the other night. I dreamt I was talking over the fence to Gladys, asking her for a bit of brown veiling to trim a hat. She said yes, she'd be glad to oblige. She went inside and came back crying, saying Fred was stretched out dead on the kitchen floor and would I come in and lay him out as she didn't fancy the job. I didn't fancy it either, but I said, Seeing you've been so obliging in the matter of the brown veiling, I suppose I can't refuse.'

'Fred looked healthy enough when I saw him last. That was Thursday.'

'Not for long, you can be sure. It's a predomination. Fred's not long for this world. A fool of a dream, too. I wouldn't have seen brown veiling on a hat in twenty years.'

'I wouldn't mention it to Gladys, if I were you.'

'I wouldn't think of it. I'm a sensitive. I see many a thing that I wouldn't mention to the person concerned.'

'I hope you haven't been dreaming about me. Have another slice of cake, Isobel?'

Isobel inquired of her stomach, whether it had recovered from Mrs Prendergast's dream. It could manage another slice of cake.

Mrs Prendergast horrified, yet Isobel persisted in listening. In her mind there was a cold collector intent on information at all costs. She was a collector of useless objects and Mrs Prendergast was one of them.

Typing classes were misery. Shorthand was not so bad; she could see the sense of shorthand. Also, the students of shorthand worked in groups, taking dictation from a teacher – one didn't have time to get to know anyone, but one didn't work in a dehumanising solitude. She excelled, so moved quickly from group to group – a sustaining experience.

In the typing class she sat at the hated machine with a wooden hood covering hands and keys (why grope when one had eyes?), forcing her fingers into an unnatural poise to lend strength to the little fingers she would well manage without (why not make typewriters to suit hands, instead of forcing hands to suit typewriters?), timing her efforts by the second hand of the large clock on the wall, pestered by the incoherent rattling of keys, while other damned souls round her competed in solitude against themselves, and thinking that this was a reasonable presentation of Hell. Devout gratitude to Aunt Noelene was all that kept her from getting up and running wildly away.

When she got back to the boarding house, walking down the side path and through the back door to avoid the dining room, Mrs Bowers would call from the kitchen, 'Is that you, Isobel? I've kept your sweets.'

This roused conflicting feelings: warmth and gratitude – it was astonishing to be remembered – but uneasiness, because she felt more return was needed than she could give. It was different from the Saturday afternoons when she was a passive listener; response was needed. But mostly, listening was sufficient, since her mouth was full of custard tart, jellied fruit or apple pie, so that she could only nod.

The information she got was interesting. Madge's vice was a strange religion: sitting around in their nightshirts saying Oompapa and staring at candles. 'Not in this house, I said to her. Do what you like outside but I'm not having altars and such stuck up in your bedroom. Doesn't do any harm though, I suppose.' (Better, no doubt, than the Other Thing.)

Betty had been the guilty party in a scandalous divorce.

'Love letters printed in the newspapers, everyone reading her business, lost the lot, house and children, left without a penny, and after all that, His Lordship stays with his wife and leaves her high and dry. Making the same mistake again by the look of it. Some women are like that; where they tripped once, they'll trip again.'

Mrs Bowers sighed painlessly over human folly as she poured Isobel a cup of tea.

Mr Watkin's great undertaking was a stud book. He followed and recorded the fortunes of dynasties of race horses. 'He has his little bet, never too much. He's a quiet, steady fellow, a real gentleman.'

Isobel, as she listened, tried on each life to see how it would suit her. Not to be the fool of love, never! Madge's life had its charm – she could see the attraction of a small, exclusive religion; the trouble was, bringing oneself to believe in it. Madge worked in the morning in the boarding house, cleaning and laundering, she went out to do the marketing, she worked in the afternoons and some evenings as a doctor's receptionist. She might need a religion. But needing it didn't provide it.

It was Mr Watkin's life that approached her ideal, the private room, the cabin furnished with pieces of one's own choosing. Work and good weather, that was all it needed. Mr Watkin strolled down the street after breakfast to buy his morning paper, came back and sat on the back verandah to read it very thoroughly, did the crossword, came to lunch, retired to his room to listen to his wireless, looked forward to his game of bridge but could endure to be disappointed of it, was calm, self-contained and self-sufficient. But one needed work, some substitute for Mr Watkin's stud book.

Going to Business College had brought her the pleasure of eating out. Sitting in the café eating fish and chips with her book open beside the plate, reading, at ease, nobody caring, she felt, for the first time she could remember, really at home.

She enjoyed the experience so much that she extended it to Saturday. At the office, one worked either Thursday evening or Saturday morning. It was always Saturday for Isobel because of the Business College, but she did not mind that. She finished work at twelve, changed her books at the library and swung happily down George Street towards the Glebe. Stopping for sandwiches and coffee was an extravagance, since she could have gone back to the boarding house for lunch, but Aunt Noelene had allowed for a little fun, and this was her idea of fun, although probably not Aunt Noelene's. She found a coffee shop at the top of Glebe Road, stayed for an hour reading in University Park, then walked back to the boarding house, paid a courtesy call on the two Fates in the kitchen, then went upstairs to read in her room, alone and at ease again. On Saturdays it seemed easy to live happily.

Rita was engaged to be married. She came into the typists' room on Monday morning in the wake of her outstretched left hand, drawn along in a dream by the diamond ring on her finger. Her friend Nell ran to hug her, Olive came to admire the ring; Isobel followed, wondering what to say. She knew one didn't congratulate the girl, one was supposed to congratulate the man; she didn't like to say, 'Good Luck!', though she meant it – in the face of Rita's drunken happiness, the thought that luck was necessary gave pain. Finally, she too admired the ring, though it seemed an odd thing to do.

They heard Mr Walter's step.

Olive said, 'You can tell us all about it at lunch time.'

They took to their desks and uncovered their typewriters. Rita was too happy to eat lunch. In the showroom, where the staff ate their sandwiches at a corner table, she waltzed, hands clasped before her, gazing into the eyes of her engagement ring, singing, 'Oh, how we danced . . .', tipsy with love.

'Hey, mind the glasses!' said Frank. 'There's not a man on earth worth a dozen stemmed cut crystal.'

Isobel said, 'My landlady doesn't think there's a man worth one small moulded liqueur glass.'

'Ah! She'd be the one with the chip!'

Everyone laughed. Even Olive. They were all enlivened by Rita's beautiful absurdity.

'If you knew my Stephen! My Stephen is worth more than all the glasses in the world!' She was off again, spinning slowly away from them and returning.

'Practising the bridal waltz,' said Frank.

'That's right. You're all coming to my wedding, girls, and who's going to catch the bouquet? Who's going to be next? Olive?'

Olive shook her head sadly. She and her boyfriend had been going out for six years; they could not marry because of family problems.

'Nell?' Nell blushed and hung her head. It seemed likely that she would be next.

'Isobel! I bet Isobel has something tucked away. You never can tell with the quiet ones.'

Isobel sighed. 'If Mr Richard doesn't speak soon, I'll have to ask him his intentions.'

Frank's mood changed suddenly. 'Laugh, clown, laugh!' he said angrily. 'Why don't you boot him?'

'Who? Me with my little number fours?'

Olive said gently, 'Mr Richard is a member of the family, Frank.'

'Big deal.' Frank was still angry.

Olive chose to ignore him.

'When do you plan to be married, Rita?'

'In September. We don't want a long engagement. Stephen's firm are sending him to Melbourne and we want to be married and go together.'

Isobel heard this with dismay. This was the opportunity Aunt Noelene would expect her to grasp, seizing that wild horse money by the bridle as it passed. She lacked courage for the deed. If she did manage it, she would have to take dictation from Mr Walter instead of checking invoices with Frank. This was life: no sooner had you built yourself your little raft and felt secure than it came to pieces under you and you were swimming again.

'Well, come on, Bel.' Frank was still sulky. 'We'd better get back to work.'

'I should like a word with Isobel, Frank,' Olive said

with dignity. 'I won't keep her long.'

Frank shrugged, unsurprised. It seemed that he had been sulking in advance.

Rita and Nell went back to their typewriters.

Olive said earnestly, 'Isobel. It really isn't right for you to be so familiar with Frank. It's a pity you've been thrown together so much. Apart from anything else,' she paused to summon her courage, 'Frank is a Communist. He has been warned, not to mention this in the office . . .'

'He hasn't mentioned it to me.'

'And another thing. If you wouldn't laugh so much at Mr Richard. I know he can be difficult, but . . . these things are more important than you think.'

'What am I supposed to do? Cry?'

Olive sighed over the difficulties of life.

'You could have Rita's job when she goes, you know. Now that you have shorthand and typing you'll be in line for a big promotion. If only you will just . . . Mr Walter is happy with your work, but he does have some doubts about your attitude. It is best to be straightforward, isn't it, in a case like this?'

Olive pleaded for approval.

Isobel said briefly, 'Thanks. I'd better get back to work.'

'Oh, ho!' said Frank. 'Who's in a nasty little temper, eh? Been warned off me, have you?' He put on a confidential air. 'Frank is a Communist.'

'They want more than they pay for.'

'Come on! Who doesn't? You just worked that one out?'

'And you have to put up with it!'

Frank gave a little rein to his own temper. 'The trouble with people like that Olive is that they don't only put up with it, they like it. They're the ones who make me sick.'

'I didn't think it would be like this. I thought you would do your work and take your money and that would be that.'

'Speaking of taking our money, I suppose we'd better get on with the work.' He had levered open a large packing case and begun to feel through the packing straw. He paused and said, 'Bel?'

'Yes?'

'What do you want out of life? I mean, it stands to reason, doing your work and taking your money isn't enough. It isn't enough for anyone, let alone you. Now, it isn't home and kids; you're not out to please the boys, or you wouldn't be pulling that nice little face around making funny remarks.'

Isobel felt deep astonishment at the words 'nice little face'.

'Just as well too, I would say. You got a long way to go before you think about that. Do you ever think about being a writer?'

'What made you think of that?'

'Well. No need to bite my head off! You nearly made me drop a week's wages.' He brushed the packing away from a moulded iridescent fruit bowl and set it on the table.

'1 – 324 Fruit Bowl iridescent one only.'

'Check.'

'I'm sorry I snapped.' She could offer no explanation either for the panic reaction.

'Well. You have this way of putting things. I thought of it when you said that about your little number fours. Summed it up in six words and made me mad, what's more. Made Olive madder, I'm thinking. Everyone can't do that.'

'I wish you'd drop it, Frank.'

'OK. But, to come back to it, what *do* you want out of life? What do you want to be? If you say Mr Walter's secretary, I'll award myself a big horse laugh.'

'I want to be one of the crowd.'

Frank got his horse laugh after all.

'That'll be the day. It'll be some crowd. You'd better start looking.'

'1 – 325. Footed compote.'

'Check. Awful stuff this is. No pleasure in it. About the Communism, I used to shoot my mouth off at work, preaching a better world to all. They told me to stop. OK. I like my job and it's their premises. But if you want to know anything about the Party, off the premises, I'll be glad to oblige, because I think it just might be the right thing for you.'

'Thanks, Frank. 1 – 329, crystal-backed mirror, comb and brush.'

'Lord preserve us. And here they are, all right. Large as life and twice as horrible.'

Two Saturdays later, the special crowd appeared. She was reading and drinking coffee in one of the booths that lined the wall of the coffee shop in Glebe Road when a group of six young people came in, greeted the proprietor and began moving chairs and pushing tables together. She was irritated at first by the noise they made as they settled themselves, and concentrated more firmly on *The Prime Minister*.

One of the young men spoke to the whole group.

'I've finished my assignment for Joseph. A neat little thing, I think.'

He made an exaggerated throat-clearing noise that commanded the attention of the others, and Isobel's, too, though she kept her eyes on her book.

'Said Auden to Spender,
"I'm just a weekender,
My boy, on Parnassus,
While you're a commuter.
Will you be my tutor?'

'Said Spender to Auden,

"Apply to George Gordon,
Most fluent of asses,
The facile Lord Byron.
Then he'll be the siren
And you'll be the warden
To cozen the masses." '

Among the laughing voices, a light, precise one cried
angrily, 'Unfair! Unfair to Auden!'

Unfair to Byron, thought Isobel angrily. Orden? Spender?
Who were they? Daring to sneer at Byron! So many
sensations swept over her at once – since the first moment
of hearing verse spoken aloud as if it was part of the
conversation, she felt her head swimming in amazement
and had to hold to her anger for support.

She looked at them then. The young man who had cried,
'Unfair to Auden!' was short and thickset; his large head
was crowned with deep glossy eaves of black hair, his small
neat features made him look like a small landscape in a
heavy frame. He was writing now, while the other one
watched, wearing a droll, wary look.

'Said Spender to Auden,
"I couldn't afford an
Apprentice so gifted.
I'd find myself lifted
To the empyrean,
So I'd rather be an
Admirer than . . ."

'Damn, I've lost your rhyme scheme.'

'Lost your rhyme too, I think.'

'There's something wrong with your rhyme scheme. Give
me your copy a minute.'

That was living as she longed to know it. Did they know

how lucky they were? Probably not. The lucky ones never did.

'Look after it, then, I want it for Joseph.'

They stirred, making room for the waitress with the coffee.

Isobel had seen one of the girls before somewhere. She was tall and beautiful, with a calm, diamond-hard, golden-skinned face and fair hair falling in an elegant sweep. School. The hair had hung in plaits then.

The other girl, the dark-haired one, spoke in a soft pleasant voice. 'Are you really going to give it to Joseph?'

'Of course I am. A commentary on Auden's *Letter to Lord Byron*. One thousand words, but I'm offering quality instead of quantity.' He looked virtuous. To say that his face was expressive still made too little of the expression and too much of the face, which, however, came almost to rest, delicate-ugly and childlike, when he added complacently, 'Joseph will say, "That's very nice, Kenneth. Now bring me the other nine hundred and fifty words. By Friday."'

His air of repose tormented Isobel, so that she realised her anger came not from loyalty to Byron, but from jealousy.

'You should have another line at the end of the first verse, it ought to go aabccb, and you've got an extra line in the second verse.'

What was the girl's name?

'Ah well, it was just a trifle, tossed off . . .'

The dark girl said, 'In the hope of dodging a bit of work. You'd have done better to write your thousand words.'

'I'll just think of a good story. The inequality of the stanzas is deliberate, as I am imitating the style of each writer . . .'

'Are you making out that Spender is wordier than Auden? What a lie!'

'Well, the extra length of the second verse gives more force to Spender's indignation. How about that?'

If Isobel could remember the girl's name she would go up to her and claim acquaintance. Though the prospect frightened her, she would do it.

'It won't do you any good with Joseph.'

'I know that, but it's fun trying.'

The other poet said, in a voice that scratched with annoyance, 'What you don't understand, Kenneth, is that Auden's so much at home on Parnassus, he can go about in shirt-sleeves and slippers. Don't underrate him because he doesn't dress for dinner.'

It was the name of Joseph – the loved, respected authority – and the affection with which Kenneth pronounced it, that cracked Isobel's matchbox cabin and sent it sliding towards the black pit.

'I think,' said the dark girl, 'that you're being a bit hard on poor old Byron. Granted that he's facile, he's done a few good things. What about *Don Juan?*' She pronounced it Wahn.

'Oh, yes,' said Kenneth. With a condescending tone, a careless movement of the hand, he turned ridicule from Byron onto himself. 'I don't condemn him utterly.'

'How kind.' The girl smiled, showing long, quite ugly teeth.

The beauty was bored. She appeared to be wondering how she had come to be there. How happy Isobel would have been in her place! If she could only remember her name . . . Hullo, Oats; Hullo Barley . . . Vinnie. Vinnie Winters.

The squat young man pushed his copy back to Kenneth, drank his coffee quickly, put a coin in the middle of the table and said, 'I'll be off, then.'

When he had gone, the dark girl said, 'You've upset Mitch!'

Kenneth grinned and chanted softly, 'Where he cannot dom-in-ate, He will not part-i-ci-pate.'

'Mitch wears a dinner jacket,' she said thoughtfully.

'Oh, yes. Mitch wears a dinner jacket. Exquisitely beaded, too.'

They laughed. Three of them laughed.

'But no spangles. Be fair.'

'Oh, no. No spangles.'

The young man on the other side of Vinnie Winters was beautiful, too, his face as diamond-hard as hers but pale, his eyes dark blue, his hair black and his features neatly insolent. The sight of him nearly destroyed Isobel's courage, yet she managed to get to her feet, walk across and say, 'You're Vinnie Winters, aren't you? We were at school together. Isobel Callaghan.'

The beauty's face, already glittering with bad temper, did not change.

'Perhaps you remember my sister Margaret. She was in your year.'

'Oh.'

Isobel was regretting her boldness when the deer-like young man opposite, reacting against Vinnie's rudeness, stood up and pulled back Mitch's chair. 'Are you alone? Come and join us. Take a seat, do. I'll get your things.' He brought her handbag and her book across, smiling over the Trollope.

Silence fell, heavily.

Kenneth said at length, 'If you were a part of speech, what part of speech would you be?' He added, blowing on his fingernails in self-congratulation, 'I speak as a verb, a transitive verb. And Janet there is a conjunction, a co-ordinating conjunction.' He turned to Vinnie. 'And you, my pet, are an adjective, naturally.' Seeing the necessity, he added, 'You adorn. You decorate.'

If the compliment had been a coin, Vinnie would have been testing it with her teeth.

'And Trevor there is a noun.'

The young man beside Isobel said, laughing, 'I would

have thought myself a verb. In the passive voice, perhaps. Well, then, an abstract noun. I'm not sure, Kenneth, that I care to have you reading my entrails, as if I were a sacred bird.'

Isobel laughed, too.

He looked at her kindly.

'And what are you?'

She said in a racked whisper, 'I think I'm a preposition.'

'Oh? Do you govern?'

'Only small common objects.'

The girl, Janet smiled at her. That was astonishing.

'I wish I could govern small common objects. Like my latch key.'

Kenneth looked at her sharply.

'To or for, by, with or from?'

The question, if not hostile, was at least challenging. She was not to be so easily accepted.

'Oh, come,' said Trevor. 'You didn't specify for anyone else.'

Isobel said on a bubble of laughter, 'My landlady's a preposition. Against.'

That brought a laugh from them all, even a smile from Vinnie. Isobel felt a little guilty, knowing she would be accepting tea, cake and kindness from Mrs Bowers later in the afternoon. She hadn't intended malice, either, but she knew she would do as much again, offer up anything that made them laugh. Making them laugh might make her acceptable.

Janet said to Kenneth, 'You may be transitive, but I'm damned if I think you're finite.'

That jolted him. His mock offence concealed true offence. She ought to sympathise with that. But what did Janet mean? Object, no subject. How clever they were.

Now Kenneth was staring insolently. 'I don't object to claiming infinity.'

'What am I?' asked the young man beside him.

There was a flash of satisfaction in Kenneth's eye at having drawn the question.

'You, Nick? You're an adverb.' He began to sing. 'It ain't what you do . . . It's de way dat you do it . . .' He laughed loudly. 'And Diana is a past participle.'

Nick grinned briefly. Trevor started and looked shocked.

Janet said, 'Vinnie, have you made up your mind about the dance?'

Vinnie shrugged, 'It's all right with me.'

'Kenneth?'

'If Vinnie has made up her mind, she has made up mine.'

'That'll be the day.'

'It is the day,' said Kenneth gently, so that she smiled.

'We're getting up a party for the Arts Ball. What about it? Trevor?'

Trevor shook his head. 'In my present delicate financial condition, no.'

'Nick?'

Nick had lit a cigarette and was now tearing unused matches one by one from the folder and dropping them in the ashtray. He shook his head without looking up.

Kenneth said, 'He is faithful to his motorbike.'

'No sidecar?'

'Positively no sidecar.'

Nick smiled at that. It seemed that Kenneth and Janet were pleased by the smile.

Janet returned to the game.

'Speaking of parts of speech, some people would just be expletives.'

Kevin laughed. 'Dr Owens!'

'Millie Turner!'

'I can offer you a personal pronoun, first person singular, in the nominative case, and a personal pronoun, first personal singular, in the objective case.'

Janet said, 'But that's all of us, isn't it? We'd be either the one or the other.'

Kevin shrugged. They were growing bored with the game. When she knew them better, she understood that boredom was their common problem. When silence fell, it weighed on them.

She got up, said to Vinnie, 'It was nice to see you again,' – and so it had been, though not for Vinnie's sake.

She walked to the boarding house entranced, full of wonder at hearing her own language spoken in a foreign city. If she never saw them again, she would know, still, that that was possible.

Mrs Bowers called her into the kitchen.

'Been out with Emma, have you? How is she?'

'Oh, quite well.'

'Sit down and I'll get you a cup of tea. How's your cup, Mrs P.?'

Isobel the born liar was back. She had crept in unnoticed when Mrs Bowers had first greeted her with 'Where have you been?'

'Having lunch with a girlfriend.'

'That's nice!'

Mrs Bowers was gratified that every life should have its pleasures. Emma was a plant she kept watered with her interest, so that it grew and flourished. Isobel had met her at Business College. (One didn't meet anyone at Business College. Business College was strictly business.) She came from the country, ('Oh, somewhere out West, I think.' – Isobel's knowledge of the country was limited.) She was going back there as soon as Isobel found the nerve to kill her off. Emma was a grievous discouragement, for there was to be no place for lying in the beautiful room. That was the disadvantage of being a born liar – one lied without thinking, rolled where one had the bias. She had felt that a taste for solitude was something to be hidden, so Emma had sprung up on cue.

In Mrs Prendergast a memory was surfacing.

'I had a cousin Emma. Second cousin that is. Got put away for a while, poor girl.'

'How was that?'

'Went very funny after the baby was born. Not the first one either, the third. Joe that would have been, got grown-up sons himself now. She was very bad for a while. She came out of it all right in the end.'

'I'm glad to hear that.' Mrs Bowers' tone admitted that Mrs Prendergast was not often the bringer of good news.

'It can take you in funny ways. There was the woman lived opposite us in Mudgee. Six weeks old the baby was and they were getting ready to go out. Her husband called out from the door, "Are you coming, Dorrie?" "I won't be a minute, dear. I'm just popping the baby in the oven." He came running in and there was the baby greased all over and trussed up in the baking dish and the oven hot. He just got to it in time.'

Mrs Bowers shrieked, 'Oh, my God!'

Isobel, who had been carrying a piece of cake to her mouth, put it down on her plate. Usually, Mrs Prendergast's plaintive but placid tone removed her memories and forebodings out of the range of human feeling; this time Isobel was seized with such anguish for the unsuspecting object in the baking dish that she wanted to run away, did not know what she was doing in this kitchen, which now seemed subterranean.

'How's that old fool in the office? Still getting on your nerves?'

'It was bad for a while when I started touch typing. I was so slow. They told me at the College not to type with two fingers and I stuck to that.'

'That's the way. Show him he can't have it all his own way.'

She had discovered also how little Mr Richard counted in the office. To be prepared to endure him was a virtue.

'My aunt's paying for the lessons, so I have to do my best. I'm typing faster now and the translation gets easier all the time because the same words keep coming up. He doesn't have much chance to complain.'

She was speaking absently, still involved with the baby in the baking dish.

'You're a clever little thing, aren't you?'

'Tell that to Mr Richard!'

That was a reasonable exit line. She put her cup in the sink, said, 'Thanks for the tea,' and was off.

All the week she thought of the group in the café. She went to the City Library looking for Orden, in vain, then skipped shorthand (but not typing) to get to the Public Library. There must be such a poet. It could not all be dream. She felt sure that if she found the poet, she would find the group again.

At last she remembered the name of the other poet – Spender! 'Said Orden to Spender – I'm just a weekender . . .' She found the name Spender in *Studies in Modern Verse*. 'Unlike W. H. Auden, Stephen Spender . . .' Auden. Once found, never lost again. It was like meeting Joseph, though Auden belonged to everyone, like God and Shakespeare, her Joseph only to her. On the other hand, Auden did exist, whereas Joseph . . . he had grown in her mind already: tall, understanding, severe and loving. It would never do to set eyes on the real one – she imagined what he might be like, a little whimsical man, plump and spry, with a bald skull and wisps of fair hair, a neat pot under a tight waistcoat . . . she was making him as unattractive as possible, out of sheer jealousy.

Next Saturday she was early at the café, reading *Can*

You Forgive Her? with less attention than usual and trying not to watch the door.

Trevor came in with Nick, looked across at her booth and called, 'Hello! It's the Trollope fancier. Come and join us!'

When she had arrived at the table, he added, 'I know you're a preposition, but I don't know your name.'

'Isobel. Isobel Callaghan.'

'I'm Trevor and this is Nick, as I suppose you've gathered.' He looked at her book. 'You are a Trollope fancier, aren't you? What are you going to read when you run out of Trollope?'

'I wish I knew.'

'What about George Eliot? Have you tried her?'

She made a face. '*Silas Marner.*'

'Oh, I know. Second Year English. A beastly little red book with gold lettering down the back. Don't be put off by that. You try *Middlemarch*. You'll be surprised! And perhaps George Meredith. You may hate him, but it's a thought.'

Janet and Kenneth came in together, arguing about an essay topic.

'But you can't call it fear in a handful of dust just because Eliot's invoking death . . .'

'Positively fond of it, wasn't he?' said Trevor.

Eliot?

They sat down and nodded to Isobel without surprise.

Trevor said to her, 'How's the Leader of the Opposition? Your landlady?'

'She's not exactly the Leader of the Opposition. That's Mrs Prendergast. Mrs Bowers is only against men. Mrs Prendergast is against the lot. She's fond of death,' she dared, 'like Eliot.'

'Fear in a handful of dust?'

'I wouldn't call her a handful of dust. More like fear

in a bowl of whipped cream.' Oh, how she tried! She told the story of Mrs Prendergast's dream, working hard at the bland, dreaming tone. She must entertain, she must be a success. 'A fool of a dream, too. I wouldn't have seen brown veiling on a hat in twenty years.'

Kenneth stopped laughing to say, 'You made that up!'

Janet said, 'I'd hate to think that she could.'

'Oh, no, not the dream. Who could, except the mind that dreamed it? No, the curlicue. The brown veiling. Did you make it up?'

She shook her head.

'You don't invent such things, Kenneth,' said Janet. 'They only happen.' She turned a troubled look on Isobel. 'Are you alone in that place?'

'Oh, no. There are four other boarders and Madge. That's Mrs Bowers' daughter. She belongs to a religious sect. They sit around in their nightshirts saying "Oompapa".'

Trevor and Kenneth exclaimed together in delight, 'Om mani padme hum.'

'Om, the jewel is in the lotus. Amen,' intoned Kenneth.

Isobel, who had been intoxicated by their attention, was seized with rage and bent her head to hide it.

Trevor saw the disturbance and took it to be shame at ignorance exposed.

'It's a Buddhist mantra,' he said. 'Buddhists in Glebe! What a thought!'

Isobel raised her head, shocked by her rage and baffled by it, too.

'What does it mean?' asked Janet.

'The jewel is in the lotus.' Kenneth said, 'I don't want to know what it means. I like it just as it is.'

'The individual is enshrined in the universal,' said Trevor. 'Sorry to spoil your fun, Kenneth.'

'You're not spoiling mine,' said Janet. 'I still don't know what it means. Kenneth, what about the ball? Are you bringing Vinnie or do we find another girl?'

There was a pause.

His face flayed with rage, his eyes cold as stones, Kenneth recited deliberately:

'I went to Belmont, where I chose
The golden casket. It contained
A vulgar message in bad prose.
I shut the box. The words remained.'

He was calm again, then. The others were silent, subdued by his moment of malevolence.

Isobel could hear Frank saying, 'Get your lubberly frame out of my living space,' and wondered if the vulgar message was anything like that. For a moment she was afraid she might laugh.

But Kenneth had Joseph.

'Well,' Janet said with shaky lightness, 'It's very neat but I hope you don't think of publishing it.'

Kenneth retreated to comedy. He said loftily, 'I do not yet know what I may see fit to do.'

Isobel could see now why Janet had said he was transitive but not finite. Objects but no subject.

He was telling a story now, face dressed and dancing, hands massaging the air. 'So I said to him, "Sir, why not devote a lecture to Ford? Don't you think Ford's work is a summary of the Elizabethan passions?" "Mr Lyne, I have devoted my last two lectures to the works of Ford." '

Ford? Eliot, Ford?

Kenneth had hung his head in pretty confusion.

'Oh, you are a lazy devil,' said Janet affectionately.

Isobel resented the affection and disliked herself for it.

Trevor walked with her down Glebe Road as far as the corner where she turned for the boarding house.

'Why didn't you go to University?'

'I have to earn my living.'

'Rotten luck.'

She didn't think so. There was more meaning in 'I have to earn my living' than the surface showed. Her forty-two and six a week and the ability to earn it were fundamental. Besides, their talk of essays, theses and assignments roused no envy.

'Not really. I only want to read books. I don't want to have to write about them.'

It was easy to talk to Trevor because he was more like a teacher than a young man.

She had given him cause to reflect.

'You're quite right, of course. Literature should be a gentleman's pleasure, not a hack's employment. Well, gentlemen are born and so are hacks.'

He sounded rueful. Could she have offended him?

But at the corner he said, 'See you next week, then?'

She nodded and went on, elated.

She was really alive now. She went off on Sundays to the Public Library looking for the writers they talked about, read Eliot and Auden, Spender and MacNeice, stayed away from the kitchen, lied without conscience to Mrs Bowers, lived for Saturdays, but lived through them and looked back on them with a strange mixture of feelings. She was really alive and morally as bad as ever.

She said to Joseph – in bed at night she humped her pillow to the shape of a shoulder and unpacked her thoughts for Joseph – 'Suppose one is born bad – not by choice – the hand of the potter shook, you might say – why can't one choose to be different? I thought I could. I thought I could make my life into a room and choose what came into it. I was a bit above myself, wasn't I? That's what monks and nuns do, with God and prayer and fasting and all that stuff. No job for an amateur.

'Besides, life isn't like that. It's more like swimming in a sea, with currents and undertows carrying you where you don't want to go.'

The currents and the undertows were mysterious evil passions, rage and envy; most of all an unconquerable sadness – no matter how willingly they accepted her – at being somehow disqualified, never to be truly one of them.

'It's envy I feel for Kenneth, all right. Because of you. Because he has the real Joseph. I know it's all nonsense; I know the real Joseph is nothing like you, but there it is. Why should I be angry with Madge?'

She could not forget that painful moment when Oompapa had revealed itself as a Buddhist mantra and an object of veneration.

'Because she keeps a stolid countenance and chews each mouthful thirty-two times? Squalid, that is. Because she knew something I didn't know? I don't really believe that's my weakness.

'This takes me back, love. Examinations of conscience. In my religious days, that was how I coped with being born bad. I put all my money on a deathbed repentance. I had all my sins named and listed ready for the moment. But the list got too long so I stopped believing in Hell instead. Ah, Joseph. My love, Joseph.'

Madge had a lover. Madge was engaged to be married. She came into the dining room one evening at supper time, leading a strange man and said, in a clear, carrying voice, 'Will you come in for a moment, Mother? I want you to meet Arthur. We are engaged to be married.'

Before Mrs Bowers appeared, there was a pause long enough for an exchange of glances, enough to examine Arthur, a short, tubby man with wild blond hair, light prominent eyes and a beautiful Grecian profile.

Mrs Bowers came to the kitchen door wearing a meek, silly look and gazed at him with wonder.

He fished for her hand, shook it and then did not know what to do with it. At last he lowered it to her side, smiling fiercely.

'Very glad to meet you,' he said breathlessly.

It might be anxiety that made his eyes seem prominent.

Mrs Bowers nodded, turned and went back into the kitchen.

Betty sprang up, took Madge by the elbows and kissed her on both cheeks.

'I'm very happy for you, my dear.' She put out her hand to Arthur. 'Congratulations! I know you're going to be very happy.'

'Thanks.'

Arthur's eyes settled. He looked as if he had run a mile.

Mr Watkin was shaking his hand now and the boys were waiting their turn.

Isobel said truthfully, 'I like your ring.'

It was a dark glowing striped stone in a heavy setting of gold.

'It's a hybrid stone. Cornelian mostly but the stripes are tiger eye and ironstone. Arthur brought it with him from the Northern Territory. I don't intend to wear it on this finger after we're married. We'll both wear plain gold bands. I'll wear this on my other hand.'

Isobel swallowed. She never disliked Madge more than when she was doing the very thing Isobel would have done in her place.

'You'll have a cup of tea with us?' said Betty to Arthur.

'We just called in, you know, to give the news.'

'Oh, you must stay. I'll get the cups.'

Betty's eyes levelled with Madge's, delivering a message. She went into the kitchen and came back carrying two cups on their saucers and wearing a little tuck of satisfaction at each corner of her mouth.

'I'll let you pour, Madge. I suppose you know how Arthur takes his tea. Now tell us all about it. When are you going to be married?'

This was a scene being played, of which Isobel did not know the meaning. Why was Betty playing hostess? Why did she look so smug? Where was Mrs Bowers? She said to herself, I sound like a serial in *Women's Own*. (Now read on . . .)

When they had finished supper, Betty was still playing the hostess. She said to Isobel, who was stacking the used cups and plates on the tray, 'Don't bother. I'll do that.'

As if the kitchen were a dragon's lair and Betty the only one brave enough to go in. Mysterious.

It was a dull afternoon at the café, conversations falling flat, boredom roosting on their shoulders.

Kenneth said, 'How's your boarding house, Isobel? What's new from Aunt Ada Doom?'

This was a promotion, being asked to entertain Kenneth. She did not welcome it. She did not want to talk about the boarding house.

'Things are bad. Madge has got engaged to one of her religious crackpots and Mrs Bowers doesn't like it at all.'

'Good for Madge,' said Janet.

Things were indeed bad at the boarding house. With the offer of a cup of tea she did not know how to refuse, she was lured into the kitchen to listen to Mrs Bowers' lamentations about Arthur and Madge's folly. Arthur of course was Madge's folly.

'One of those religious crackpots. She never should have gone near them. Plenty of decent respectable religions you can take up if you're that way inclined. I told her so till I was tired of it but would she listen? No. You'd think she'd seen enough of men in her own home. And what good can you expect of a man with nothing better to do than sit around in his nightshirt spouting rubbish?' *Om mani padme hum*. Isobel still winced at the thought of it.

'I said to her, "Never mind about me. It's you I'm thinking of." Though how I'll manage alone I don't know. I didn't have to tell her not to think of me, believe me. Possessed, that's what she is. They've got her in with their mumbo jumbo. She's always been weak, poor girl. Always been a fool for any man that'll say two words to her. Last time it was a widower with four children. She saw reason about that, but there's no reasoning with her this time. Water off a duck's back. Did you see that lump of rubbish he's given her for an engagement ring? Couldn't run to a decent diamond. I always say, if a girl has a decent engagement ring, she has something of her own. Madam Betty, it was all she was left with. Worth a packet, too.'

'Of course he's not right in the head. You can tell by the look in his eyes. And I'm beginning to think she's not much better.'

The responses she drew from Mrs Prendergast gave little consolation.

'Ah, that's the way of it.'

'It's always a gamble.'

'An aunt of mine took up with the Christian Science. A very funny lot they were.'

Mrs Bowers shouted in exasperation, 'This hasn't got anything to do with your Christian Science!'

Mrs Prendergast looked jolted and affronted. She offered nothing after that but a dignified silence.

Isobel was disappointed at the frustration of Mrs Prendergast's story about the Christian Science. She was bored and embarrassed by Madge's love affair and even more by Mrs Bowers. She had nothing to offer but her presence, which she regretted. It was fortunate that Mrs Bowers could go on talking with only minimal response.

Something else was bad at the boarding house. The other boarders, except Mr Watkin, who moved like a small planet in his own atmosphere, were hostile to her now.

'Where did you get that coat, Isobel?'

Norman had studied it with insulting curiosity.

'I inherited it.'

'It looks like it.'

Betty had looked it up and down and said crisply, 'It's been a good coat in its day.'

Isobel had in return looked Betty up and down, said nothing but drawn a little blood.

'The very kind of bitchery I most detest!' she had cried that night to Joseph. 'Besides, I think she's beautiful. Her age doesn't matter. I didn't have anything to throw at her except being eighteen, and what's that? Everyone is eighteen sometime or other. But oh, Joseph, why do they hate me? If it was just the Eleventh Commandment I could bear it.' The Eleventh Commandment was *Thou shalt not be different*. 'I don't care about Norman either. Whatever is eating him he is welcome to.' She had an odd idea about what was eating Norman. She drew it from the poltergeist rages that affected him whenever Betty was away and the calm her return brought him. He thought youth was too good for the likes of Isobel. But Betty. Why should Betty, who was amiable and well-mannered, though perhaps a little cold-hearted, turn on her so? 'I wanted her to like me. This is when I worry, when people dislike me and I don't know why.'

Joseph had no answer. Joseph was a listener only.

Squalor and misery at the boarding house. She was thankful for the interruption when Janet, who was facing the doorway, groaned softly, 'Oh, my God. Look who's here.'

Nick stiffened and remained quite still.

A tall dark girl with avid eyes was staring at them from the doorway.

'She's been to Fifty-one, I suppose. Helen wouldn't have told her. She must have looked in by chance. Damn.'

Kenneth had lowered his eyes against an indecency. Trevor got up, put his money on the table and hurried towards the girl. He put his arm around her waist and walked away with her.

Janet said angrily, 'No self-respect at all. None. Nick, I do think it would be better if you faced it and talked to her. If you could make her see it's no use . . .'

'I should think she knows that,' said Kenneth.

'Then what's the point?'

'Well,' he answered slowly, 'she is annoying him. That might be better than nothing.'

Nick had lit a match, let it burn down, placed it carefully between his hands and was now staring at the identical images of the burnt match that lay at the base of each thumb. The excessive innocence of his face must be hiding fierce embarrassment.

'There is not one damned thing Nick can do about it, except wait till she gets tired of it, so don't nag at him.'

To turn oneself into a weapon, to throw oneself like a stone or a rotten tomato, to be so lost – Isobel felt a keen thrill at the thought of it.

This must be Diana, the past participle. And Nick had laughed at that spiteful remark. Perhaps there had been nothing else to do.

She pitied Diana but was curious too. She wanted to know what it was like. She felt about Diana as she had felt about children who got the cane at the convent; they knew what it was like.

'Well, I suppose it's safe for you to go home, Nick,' said Janet. 'I think I'll walk around to Fifty-one too and see

Helen. Oh, what about Mitch? Wasn't he supposed to be bringing his sonnet sequence?'

Kenneth said, 'That could be another reason for going to Fifty-one.'

'I'd like to see you,' thought Isobel, 'I'd like to see you standing wrung in a doorway staring at someone you love, hopelessly.'

'He'd be here now if he was coming, I suppose. All right, then.'

Nick and Trevor lived at Fifty-one. It was a cabalistic number to Isobel.

They counted out money and split the bill.

'Are you coming, Isobel?'

After all, she thought, nobody sees into my mind. Everyone dislikes Kenneth from time to time. But nobody wants to miss a word he says, and that includes me.

Now they were on their way to Fifty-one, Janet subduing the energy of anger to a casual stroll, the young men walking ahead, Isobel looking with wonder at the back of Nick's head, picturing the beautiful calm face which hid vulnerability, confusion, helplessness.

Down Glebe Road, to the left instead of the right, another turning into a street of large houses set in gardens. Number Fifty-one was as ornamental as an old-fashioned sideboard. The heavy front door bore a bright brass knocker; stained glass panels at either side glowed dull ruby and emerald.

'It's Helen's house,' Janet explained. 'She wanted to hang on to it when her parents died, so she lets rooms to keep it going.'

Nick opened the door, looked at them with apology, and went up the stairs.

Janet muttered, 'God, how she bugs him. If she would just leave him alone . . .'

Kenneth nodded, looking after Nick with a frown of worry that made him, for a moment, endearing.

'Oh, well. Better go and say hullo to Helen.'

She led them down the hall into a large kitchen where a dark, stocky woman sat at the table reading. She looked up and said, 'Hullo. I thought Nick and Trevor were with you.'

'They were.' Janet took a chair. Kenneth sat on the edge of the table. Isobel stood waiting, till the young woman smiled at her and said, 'Take a seat.'

'Oh. This is Isobel. Helen. Nick's gone upstairs. We had a visitor at the café.'

'Oh God. I didn't tell her where you were. I don't say I wasn't tempted. What a bind she is, the poor girl.'

'Poor girl. Poor Nick, you mean.'

Kenneth said, 'She's got to give up sometime. I think.' He brightened. 'Perhaps Trevor will take her over. Greater love hath no man.' He giggled unlovably.

Yet the girl at the café had been beautiful, except for the obsessed eyes. How dreadful, to be a corpse before you died, with the flies buzzing about you, buzzing 'no self-respect', 'what a bind'. The flies enjoying it, too, notwithstanding their indignation on Nick's account.

Isobel was frightened by Diana's plight, and amazed that beauty had not saved her.

The stuttering roar of a motorbike started in the yard, counterpoise to Nick's silence.

'Well, there goes Nick. Escaping.'

'I did think she'd given up,' said Helen. 'She hadn't been round for a fortnight. My heart sank, I tell you, when I heard her coming down the hall.'

What a struggle there might have been in that staying away for a fortnight, that nobody gave Diana credit for.

Janet said bitterly, 'Because she'd managed to finish things between him and Anthea; that's why she calmed down. You wait and see, she'll be as bad as ever if he takes up with anyone else.'

'It's amazing though,' said Kenneth, 'what you can get away with if you give up caring about anything else, like self-respect and pride and all that stuff. Turning yourself into a projectile, so to speak.'

This was so close to Isobel's thought that she wondered why she could not feel more sympathy with Kenneth.

Janet said, 'A new way of throwing yourself at a man's head.'

Isobel saw Nick as an exiled prince, not meant for sitting talking in cafés, driven by a fury out of his own kingdom.

'But what does she do?' she asked.

'She stands outside,' said Janet. 'She follows him and stands watching, wherever he goes. When he took up with Anthea, she followed him there and stood outside, haunting the place.'

Helen said, 'I think if Anthea had cared about him, she would have tried to weather it.'

'She didn't get time to find out if she cared for him. And nobody will, unless she gives up.'

'No followers, that's Nick,' said Kenneth, and laughed wildly. 'No followers but one.'

Janet looked at him angrily. 'It must be dreadful for him. He never says. I suppose he talks to Trevor . . .'

Trevor came in then, looking troubled and remote.

'Well, did you get her to go home?'

He nodded. 'Come and look at my books, Isobel. I probably have something you'd like to borrow.'

Trevor was asking her to come into his bedroom. She was locked in panic, with a voice screaming at her from the past, but nobody else seemed to think the invitation odd and Trevor had spoken casually – a little more casually than usual, perhaps. She got up and followed him, so nervous that she felt herself plodding across the room and clung to the bannisters on her way upstairs behind him.

'I can't lend you *Middlemarch* because I'm doing my thesis on George Eliot.'

It was probably because he didn't think of her as a girl, just as a reader, that it was all right to invite her into his bedroom.

'Well, come on in.'

He was looking at her with a particular laughing smile that was private, but not unkind. He took a cushion from the armchair and put it on the floor for her in front of the bookshelves. She turned to them as if they were home but was rebuffed by strange titles.

'What about the Russians? Have you tried Dostoevsky?'

She shook her head.

'I think you must. Start with *Crime and Punishment*. If that doesn't get you, nothing will.' He pulled out a book in the friendly red and white paper cover of the Everyman edition and handed it to her. 'And now you are going to read your way right through Dostoevsky. You little guts.'

Isobel wilted. Was that the wrong way of reading, then? It was always like this: whenever she acted without thinking, she made herself ridiculous – but what a burden, to have to think about everything . . . and where were the rules? What did she have to go by?

'And you aren't going to tell me what you think about him, either, because you don't want to talk about books.' That smile again. 'You only want to read them.' Now he was rueful. 'You stung me there, you know. I can't help thinking there's a place for the critic. Some people even call criticism an art. The artist responds to experience, the critic responds to the experience of books.'

'Is Kenneth a good poet?'

Hoping he wasn't. Oh, Isobel, why? To hope that verse was bad was a dreadful immorality.

'Very good, so far. He has the gift, all right.'

Perceiving some reserve in his voice, she said, 'Isn't that everything?'

'I don't know. I hope so. How can you be sure of anyone's coming good? It's going to be a terrible pity if he doesn't.' He added mysteriously, 'I wish Kenneth would meet the right girl.'

'What about Mitch?'

'He hasn't got as much as Kenneth but he's going to bring everything he's got to harbour.' He grinned. 'You can be sure of that.'

Isobel had forgotten her wounded feelings. How interesting this was. And he was going to lend her his books.

'You can read their stuff, if you like. Look here.' He opened the bedside cabinet. There was a stack of magazines in each of the two compartments. '*Arna* on top, *Hermes* below. Don't take them away, please, and get them out of order at your peril.'

'Would you show me something of Kenneth's?'

Downstairs, a clock chimed. One, two, three, four, five . . . not six. Surely not six. She jumped up, crying in panic, 'I must go.' She seized *Crime and Punishment*, gabbled, 'When I've finished it . . .'

'Don't worry if I'm not here. Just put it back and take *The Brothers Karamazov*.'

Mrs Bowers was going to be angry.

'Thank you. I have to run. Didn't realise the time.'

'No trouble, Cinderella.' He looked at her, shaking his head and laughing.

Why had he called her Cinderella? True, of course, but how had he known that?

Because of the clock striking, silly. Stop looking for insults where there aren't any.

Her body was hurried along on seven-year-old legs that wanted to break into a run. Glebe Road. One block, round the corner . . .

In the dining room, she slid into her place behind a cooling plate of lamb cutlets. They looked up, acknowledging her arrival, without affection.

It was always like this. She had tried, been polite, passed the salt without being asked, would have liked Betty if that had been allowed. It had not been allowed, and tonight the coolness was more marked than usual, bringing the familiar stab of fear that she had done something to offend, sharper because of the hour of peaceful excitement and self-forgetfulness in Trevor's room. Self-forgetfulness was always dangerous.

And thirty-one and thirty-two, she thought snappishly, in time with Madge's steady chewing, but could not raise her spirits. How much she wished to know where she went wrong.

While Madge was carrying plates of Sunday roast dinner from the serving hatch to the table, Mrs Bowers appeared at the kitchen door, looking angry. Anger had engraved its history on Mrs Bowers' face; when the lines it had made there came alive, the effect was frightening.

'One of you hasn't changed your bed. There's been sheets and a towel in the hall all morning, a nice thing on a Sunday. I want the beds changed straight after breakfast, please, and the used sheets in the laundry.'

Isobel cried, 'Oh, I'm sorry. They're mine.' She had got up in a hurry and made her bed before she remembered that it was Sunday. 'I'll do it straight away.'

'Oh.' She sobered, seeing that Isobel was the culprit. 'Never mind, they can stay till after dinner now.'

It was all right, then, about last night. She probably hadn't noticed that Isobel was late.

In the kitchen, she was talking angrily to Mrs Prendergast. Isobel tensed again, but there was nothing about lateness or unchanged beds. It was only about Arthur.

'Coming to live here, indeed. Easy to see what that gentleman is after. No sooner married, I suppose, than he'll find work is too much for him and he'll have his armchair in the lounge for the rest of his life.'

Deadly embarrassment stilled the diners. Knives and forks struggled heavily against it.

Madge stood up and and walked to the kitchen door. She said, as deliberately as she had chewed, 'Do you have something to say to me? If you have, say it.'

Norman clasped his hands above his head and moved arms and shoulders in a dance of joy, grinning encouragement at Madge's back. Betty looked up and smiled at him. From the kitchen, silence.

Mrs Bowers said, in an outraged voice, 'Well, if you want the whole world to know your business . . .'

Quickly, Tim filled his mouth with a crumpled paper serviette while laughter shook his torso.

Awed by Madge, Isobel thought, 'If I could ever have done that . . .'

Madge said, 'Arthur offered to come and live here because you said you could not manage without my help. If you don't want us to live here, that will suit us very well. Now, tell me what you want me to do, please. And remember that we can manage very well without you.'

Silence. Madge turned and walked out. Isobel looked with religious respect at her unfinished dinner.

Her head rang then under a hammer-blow of enlightenment.

You didn't hate Madge for her methodical mastication. You hated her because you took her place.

She had read somewhere that from the window of a plane, at the right height, on a clear day, one could see Tasmania, the whole recognisable map-shape. Now she was there, right height, right light, with Tasmania spread out below. Seeing took time. She sat, stunned, while Betty went out to the kitchen and the others scraped and stacked plates.

You left the house thinking of freedom, of being a different person, seeing the world ahead of you, but you didn't go on, you went back. To fight the old fight and this time to win, to have the verdict set aside, to be the favoured child.

Betty came back with a tray and served out canned peaches and jelly, decorous, as if at a funeral. She took the used plates, stacked them on the tray and carried them out.

Mrs Bowers' favoured child? Isobel, you don't aim very high. But that didn't matter, not at all, if you wanted what you wanted badly enough. Like power. Memory served up puny, submissive Mr Gibson, who had lived with his masterful wife across the way in Plummer Street, wearing the stern marble face of justice while he rubbed a puppy's nose in the pool of its widdle.

Any rag will make a doll for the idiot in the attic.

Auden had a general in his head. ('But they've severed all the wires, and I don't know what the general desires').

Isobel had an idiot in the attic.

She got up to help with the clearing away, abstracted but not depressed, although sobered. It was impossible to be depressed after seeing Madge walk out. That was an uplifting little miracle; it was like seeing a bone walk away from a dog. The others were feeling it, too, glowing quietly and suppressing smiles.

Back in her room, she sat on her bed and reflected. She was in a different position from Auden; she knew what the idiot desired, all right, and had to watch to see it didn't get it. This was different from Joseph, too. She knew, when she thought about the dream Joseph, that he was like a father, really, more than a lover. That was a game, if you liked (real indoor sport, couldn't be more indoor, she thought, with a grin), but she knew it was a game. It didn't tangle with the real world. Yes, at one point it did, because there was a real Joseph, and at that point it made trouble, making her sick with jealousy of Kenneth.

I ought to change your name, my dear, she thought, but she could not. There had to be one little cell of flesh to make a dream live.

Just remember why you're jealous of Kenneth and try not to hate him.

The idiot played its games with the real world and – and what was worse – it played them behind Isobel's back. Not any more, now that she knew. Could she do this, watch a part of herself and control it, fight against it all her life?

She was not too discouraged, the new knowledge giving her a feeling of strength. At least she knew where she was going wrong – no wonder the others disliked her, watching her suck up to Mrs Bowers, taking what ought to be Madge's.

Idiot wants a mother.

Idiot can't have one.

Life is very difficult.

It was quiet in the house. She heard someone come upstairs, thought she recognised Madge's step and could have howled with grief and disappointment, thinking Madge had given in and turned the splendid walkout into a feeble gesture. Then she heard Madge's voice. If Arthur was with her, there was hope. She decided on a scouting trip towards the bathroom.

The door of Madge's room was open; Madge and Arthur were packing. Isobel noted with deep admiration that they were not trying to be quiet. She approached (like a commoner sucking up to a duke, hoping some of the quality would rub off on her) and said, 'Can I do anything to help?' It wouldn't matter if she got a knockback, because she would know why.

Madge looked up from putting shoes into a carton. Her smile was beautiful.

'Thanks. If you'd go with Arthur and take this down

to the car, that would be a great help.'

Arthur too, though tubby and pale-eyed, had an aristocratic air at the moment, being full of triumph and energy. He lifted a suitcase gaily and led the way downstairs.

Isobel was afraid – no, not Isobel, but the idiot was afraid of meeting Mrs Bowers. On the way back, she got a glimpse of a head dodging out of sight at the kitchen door and started with fear, though she told herself that it was better for Mrs Bowers to know where she stood. The trouble was that the idiot shared her body and had a hold on it.

She helped with the final load of luggage and said goodbye to Madge at the gate. Madge kissed her, a proxy kiss, she knew, but she didn't mind that. She felt she was doing something good, being there to receive it.

In the café there were only Kenneth and Mitch bent over pages of manuscript with Janet watching attentively. No matter how Kenneth had rolled his eyes at the thought of Mitch's sonnet sequence, he was reading it seriously now, stopping to smile with pleasure and say, 'A felicity!' or tap with his fingernail a passage he doubted.

The atmosphere was peaceful and buoyant, like a celestial quilting party. Janet must be feeling that too, for she smiled, as Isobel sat down quietly, and murmured, 'Trevor and Nick have gone away for the weekend. Trevor said to remind you, *The Brothers Karamazov.*'

She was glad Trevor was not there, for last week's expansive conversation had brought on a mortal shyness.

'Oh, he said too, he's astonished at you. A whole week over *Crime and Punishment*. Are you losing your appetite?'

What did that mean? Did she read too fast, too slowly? Fortunately, she need not worry about it, since she did not have to answer.

Janet said, as Kenneth put a page aside, 'May we?'

Mitch nodded. He was quietly elated by praise from Kenneth.

Having read some of Mitch's verse in *Hermes*, Isobel had slotted it into a pigeonhole and expected no revelation, but the sonnet sequence was much better than she had expected; she remembered what Trevor had said, that Mitch would bring everything he had to harbour, and was pleased that he was right.

She walked to Fifty-one in a tranquil frame of mind, and found Helen drinking coffee in the living room with a wiry young man, plain, ruddy-faced, bespectacled, brindle-haired. This must be her boyfriend, Dan, with whom she shared the large front bedroom. So Janet had said, and the knowledge made Isobel shy as she looked in on them.

'I'm just going up to Trevor's room to get a book.'

They looked up, Helen from the *New Yorker* and the young man from the *Herald* crossword and smiled so kindly, she realised she was being childish, and should have gone straight upstairs. That mortified her, but she forgot it, sitting in front of Trevor's bookshelves looking into one book after another. This was like the best hours of childhood.

The door opened and Helen came in.

'Isobel. You're still here. Look, there's Diana at the door. I saw her coming and I bolted. I can't stand another minute of it. I had her all Wednesday night, I swear she's getting worse. Go down, will you, and tell her I'm out? Everyone's out, Nick's away?'

At the front door the knocker sounded firmly, insistently, self-righteously.

'OK.' Isobel took *The Brothers Karamazov* and ran downstairs.

She opened the front door, faced Diana, said, 'Hullo.'

What an odd thing to say to that tense, unresponsive

face. 'Did you want to see Helen? I'm afraid she's out.'

Diana walked past her into the sitting room. Baffled, Isobel followed.

Diana looked about her. On the low table in front of the settee there were two coffee cups, a *New Yorker*, the *Herald*, folded to the crossword partly filled in, and a pencil lying across it. Isobel didn't know what sort of *Marie Celeste* story she could invent to explain that.

Diana sat down on the settee.

'I know they're here. They saw me coming and they cleared out. I don't blame them. I know I'm a curse and a bore.'

Shocked, Isobel thought, 'She doesn't know me. She doesn't even know my name.' A naked soul was just as shameful as a naked body.

Diana picked up the paper and ran her finger lovingly over the crossword. Thinking of plain, sandy Dan, Isobel bit her lip.

It's not funny. She's suffering.

'He was sitting here, doing the crossword.'

'Who?' Isobel thought there might be some good in reminding Diana she was a stranger.

'Nick.'

Pronouncing his name, she began to cry and had to pause to swallow her tears and dry her eyes.

'Nick was here. Nick is here. He is in this house and I can't see him. Anyone else in the world can see him, but I can't, and I'm the one person it's life or death to.'

Embarrassed as she was, Isobel couldn't help being interested in hearing these worn words take meaning, like old hulks with their sails filled out by the wind.

She said, 'Nick's not here. He's away for the weekend.'

How safe she felt, being able to pronounce the name indifferently.

Diana smiled and closed her eyes. When she opened them

she said, 'I suppose you think I'm shameless. I'm not.'

I'm a stranger, but she takes it for granted that I know about her; she knows that people talk about her. She's a corpse all right with the flies buzzing round her, and she hears them buzzing, though she's dead.

'I feel shame, all right, the way nobody else can know it. Sometimes I think it's all I ever feel. If you knew the things I've done! I've followed him to that girl's house, I've stood outside till they came out and I've followed them. I followed them to the theatre and I couldn't get a seat, so I stood outside and waited for them. If they'd got a bus, I'd have followed them but they got a taxi. I rattled them so much they had to get a taxi.' She said this with a faint sneer. If this was shame, it looked very much like arrogance. 'I did that and I did it again. Can you imagine that? I've got no pride, no self-respect left. I've got nothing. I've lost my job now, and no wonder.'

I'm a messenger, Isobel thought with resentment. I'm supposed to tell Nick she's lost her job.

She said, 'That's terrible. What are you going to do?'

Diana shook her head, smiling a faint complacent smile of despair.

'I used to think he'd come back to me when he saw how much I was suffering. Of course that never happens, but it was something I had to think. Something I had to hold on to. Now I know that he won't, but it doesn't make any difference.'

The idea of losing a job was so alarming to Isobel that she could not leave the subject. 'But what are you going to do? You have to have a job. You have to eat!'

Diana considered that idea carefully, then shrugged.

'I've got some money saved.'

'And when that's gone?'

She sounded quite belligerent. Interesting. Here was someone feeble enough to bring out the bully in Isobel.

'What do I care? I don't care about anything. I'm finished. I'm as good as dead.'

Isobel reflected. 'You know, I think that's right. I mean, if you take life as change and development – and I think it must be, life must be always changing . . . if you had a life without change, it might be as good as death, I suppose . . . well, when you can't change, I suppose you are as good as dead.'

She was so interested in this idea that she forgot Diana and spoke with detachment, then was startled at the fury in Diana's eyes. True to form, she made a note: masochists prefer to devise their own sufferings. True to form also, she retreated before anger.

'I'm not talking about you, particularly.' (But I ought to be; that's where the offence is.) 'I just meant anyone who can't adapt . . . Look, Nick's not here, truly. He's away for the weekend. Let's go. We can't go on just sitting here, can we?'

She could not leave Diana, who was looking cynically now at the coffee cups.

'It wasn't Nick doing the crossword. It was Helen and Dan. All right, they did get up and run when they saw you coming. What do you expect? They can't do anything for you.'

She was shocked by Diana's sick, stunned look and her heavy nod.

I've gone too far. I'm no good at this sort of thing. Why did I even get into it?

Diana picked up her bag and made for the door. Isobel followed. They walked abreast, but not together, up Glebe Road to the bus stop, Isobel full of misery and remorse and longing for the moment when she could take refuge with the brothers Karamazov.

At the bus stop Diana turned to her.

'Come home with me, will you? Come and have

a meal. I think you could help me.'

Oh, no, you'd eat me alive. On and on. Once you got hold of me, I'd never get away.

'I'm sorry. I can't. Not this evening.'

There had been a different look on Diana's face, a waking look. Isobel realised that as it faded.

'No, of course not. People have dates on Saturday night.' She smiled that peaceful, distant smile.

They waited in silence then till the bus came and she got on it without saying goodbye.

And now for the brothers Karamazov.

She wished Trevor would not say those puzzling things. It was so interesting to listen to him and wonderful to be able to borrow his books; why did he make these odd little remarks that made her feel awkward with him?

Back in her room, she opened the book with great anticipation, but she could not concentrate on reading at first. Diana's face with its waking look kept appearing on the page.

You shouldn't have talked to her at all if you didn't care enough to go all the way.

She might have meant it. You might have been able to help her. The turning point. Isobel the turning point. That is ego. You're kidding yourself. She lit up because she thought she had a new victim.

Victim. That's a funny word. The poor girl is suffering terribly, she's the victim. Selfish and heartless Isobel.

I did feel for her. Once or twice I felt for her very much.

You didn't act on your feelings, so that doesn't count.

The story took over at last. She read till the dinner bell sounded angrily. Since Madge had left, the boarders all seemed to be conscious of Mrs Bowers' anger glowing like a portable stove in the kitchen. It drew them closer. Betty helped with the serving, showing a domestic streak which made her seem more of a likeable duck than a daunting swan; the boys were quieter and more companionable. Isobel, who was avoiding Mrs Bowers because of the idiot in the attic, was trying again to be acceptable to the others. She said, 'I'll get the plates, Betty. You might spoil your dress.'

Mrs Bowers, dishing up at the stove, gave her a mean look that made her quail. She didn't want Mrs Bowers to like her, yet she quailed. Her body was a dog that answered to the orders of others.

She looks at everyone like that, she's in a general rage, Isobel thought, taking the first two plates, yet it was extremely difficult to go back for the others. She had meant to help with the washing up, but decided against it.

Tim said to Betty, who was wearing her good black, 'Big date tonight, Betty?'

'Yes, doing the town tonight.'

Isobel saw Diana's remote smile again. People have dates on Saturday night.

She did not read the meaning of the smile till later, in the moment before sleep, which it banished. Diana had a date too; she was going alone to that most private of all appointments. Isobel was sure of it; the peace and decision in the smile told her so.

As good as dead. You told her she was as good as dead.

What exactly did you say?

She was familiar with that question and knew there was no answer to it, but she couldn't help looking for one, over and over.

You are as good as dead. *You* are as good as dead. It was all in the stress. She hadn't meant Diana, particularly. She couldn't have been so cruel as to say that to Diana.

Oh, yes, you could, if you weren't watching yourself. The idiot in the attic is a spiteful little bastard.

This was a terrible way of passing the time, like being

made to work out one of those infinite repeater things in Maths for ever.

It doesn't matter how you said it. What matters is how Diana heard it. You could see that, all right.

You told her she was as good as dead, then you let her go home alone, though she asked you to come. That might be when she made up her mind, thinking, 'I'll ask her to come home with me.' Like tossing a coin. 'If she says no, I'll do it.'

Nobody will ever know it was me.

Oh, God! Isobel!

Abject as the thought was, she clung to it, to silence the infinite repeater, to be able to get to sleep.

Keep away from people, don't meddle in future. That was the lesson.

Every day she bought the paper to look for a paragraph headed GIRL FOUND DEAD IN FLAT.

Sometimes she was sure Diana wasn't dead, that her obsession was ridiculous. She conjured up Diana's face, looking for reassurance in it and seeing the deadly little smile again.

She wanted to go round to Fifty-one for news of Diana. She was one person who would be delighted to see Diana. She did not dare to go to Fifty-one (which existed in any case only on Saturdays), for fear of showing a special interest in the matter. That showed that she cared more about being found out than about Diana's living or dying.

They'll ask you questions, because you were the last person to speak to her. How did she look, what did she say? Did she give any indication that she was about to take her own life?

I told her she was as good as dead.

Crime and punishment. She was a twopenny Raskolnikov. She could think thoughts like that only in the moments when she believed Diana was alive. The rest of the time she was numbed by depression.

She would never speak without thinking again. She would watch every word.

Meanwhile, she began to see that Mrs Bowers was angry with her particularly. Standing at the stove with the wholesome smell of baked dinner rising round her, she glared at her, looking like a witch that has got hold of the wrong recipe. She couldn't turn such malevolence on everyone, she wouldn't have the energy for it.

Isobel accepted it passively.

'You wanted Madge's place,' she said to herself, 'and now you've got it.' She thought of Madge, leaving so splendidly, but could not imagine having so much strength, herself. It was easy to bear Mrs Bowers' dislike, now that she was prepared for it, easy to keep her head low and her eyes averted, much easier than going out into a strange world again.

At the café there was no talk of Diana, only of Mitch's sonnet sequence, which Trevor was sorry to have missed.

They would know by now if Diana was dead. Time let you off at last, as she had noticed before.

'It's not purely decorative,' Kenneth said. 'That's the interesting thing. It's full of the usual decorative bits, but there's a context. I'd like to read it again.'

Janet said, 'You've no idea how delighted Mitch was because Kenneth liked it. The air was full of the beating of angels' wings.'

Kenneth grinned. 'I hope he didn't notice how surprised I was.'

'I wish I'd been there,' Trevor said again.

'Well, it's going into *Hermes*.'

Nick wasn't there, but Nick was never really there. He was the charming exile.

Alone with Isobel on the way back to Fifty-one, Trevor

said, 'I have a weakness for reading things in manuscript. I know it's childish, but there it is.'

'I think it's exciting, too. I suppose, if you write manuscript, it's print that exciting.'

'Yes, I suppose so.'

There was a remoteness in his tone today that made her uneasy. Had she done something wrong? How much she wanted not to offend Trevor.

She asked, 'Do you write?'

He shook his head.

'Do you wish you did?' Her jaws were heavy, hard to move as she asked the personal question, but he took it calmly.

'No. What I want to be is a good critic. You know, the kind who can tell good from bad, when it's new, in a new form . . . a spotter, in fact. There aren't many. About Dostoevsky. Are you ever going to say anything about Dostoevsky? Why do I nag you? It's quite legitimate to read for reading's sake. And there's the other end of the scale, where people read books only to write about them. Yes, and people write books for other people to write theses about. Why do I complain when I meet a consumer?'

Consumer was just the word.

Her jaws were heavy again. 'It's not like reading, Dostoevsky especially. It's like living in it.'

Particularly *Crime and Punishment*.

'Um, perhaps no more Dostoevsky for the moment. We don't want you turning tragic and Russian.' He sounded positively like Joseph; she felt an intimate shame, as if he had found out about him.

'I got *Middlemarch* from the library. I haven't started it yet.'

'Dear me, you are slipping.'

She wished he would not laugh at her.

In his room he turned to face her, looking like a handsome

pale horse about to bolt, took a step towards her, said 'Isobel', and put his arms round her.

It was her body that fought, not she. It stiffened and struggled against being pushed out onto a tightrope from which it must fall. Her hands went up and pushed at his chest, pushing him away. He dropped his arms, said with a gasp of pain he managed to shape into a laugh, 'Sorry. Forget I mentioned it.' Then he walked quite wildly to his desk, sat down, opened a book and stared at it.

Nothing to be done. She put *The Brothers Karamazov* on the bed and ran away.

It was all gone in a second, the café, the books, the conversation, and she had hurt Trevor, made him gasp with pain.

Later, she thought wistfully of the vanished prospect of being Trevor's girlfriend, of belonging . . . Couldn't she have pretended? Would it have been enough, if she had done everything he wanted? That would have been no trouble; she would have been quite ready always to do what Trevor wanted. But she would have had to know what he did want. It would be like being a spy in a foreign country, having to pass for a native. She would be found out. The penalty for being found out appeared as Diana, walking and watching, obsessed with suffering. That moment when you found out they hated you and you did not know why – any deprivation was better than that.

But she had lost Joseph, too. Trevor was Joseph. She had lost them both.

Next Saturday she walked through the streets and the parks of the surrounding suburbs, feeling lonely, wondering what they were talking about at the café, telling herself it was all for the best, thinking sadly if . . . if Trevor had gone a bit slower, if she had had some warning, if he had asked her to the pictures on Saturday night (she had to laugh at the idea of Trevor's doing that) – no, it wouldn't have made any difference, she was what she was and nothing could change her, so best to be done with it.

She passed a house with a sign ROOM VACANT and thought of safety, a bolthole.

She walked into town, away from the empty streets, but town didn't offer what she needed, which was a big, cheerful carnival crowd. There were people in twos and threes, looking bored and aimless, offering no comfort.

She came in late for dinner. Mrs Bowers made a special trip into the dining room with her plate – not that she had kept it in the oven, for it was cooling and congealing – and put it in front of her with a thud. She stared down at it and began to eat, scraping away the cold, sticky gravy and eating the tepid meat, knowing the others were looking away in embarrassment.

Who cared? If Mrs Bowers knew how miserable she was, she would not be wasting her energy on puny efforts to annoy.

On Monday morning Mr Walter came into the outer office and said distantly, 'A phone call for you, Miss Callaghan.'

Her amazement, which was genuine, was also the best defence. Private phone calls at the office were unheard of. She had to walk past Mr Walter, trying to keep her composure, and pick up the phone on his desk while he watched.

'Isobel, this is Helen. You know, from Fifty-one.'

'Who gave you this number?'

'Oh, does it matter? We worked it out – your boss's name. Isobel, Nick is dead.'

'Don't be silly. How can he be dead?' How odd her own voice sounded, thin and exasperated.

'It's true. It was an accident, on his bike. A car hit him. It happened yesterday, he was badly injured. He died, just now, in the hospital. They rang to tell me, his mother's there. Look, I want you to do something for me, I want you to go and break it to Diana. It's a terrible thing to ask you, but I can't think of anyone else. Trevor's just about at the end of his tether, I can't ask him, and Kenneth and Janet . . . they aren't sympathetic, Janet's got some crazy idea that Diana is to blame, I don't know what they might say to her. I know it's a lot to ask . . .'

'I can't go now, I don't get off work till five o'clock.'

A hand touched her arm. She looked up. Mr Walter, looking gentle, was nodding.

'It's all right.'

She echoed into the phone, 'It's all right. I can go now.'

'Oh, that's good. It's his mother, you see. She's at the hospital, she'll be coming here to get his things – I can't have Diana round here making scenes. It's all bad enough.'

'What's the address?'

'Lucky, we found that, in the telephone book. Nick must have written it in. It's Kirribilli.'

'Wait on.'

A notebook and a gold propelling pencil appeared by her hand.

'Flat 7, 34 Mount Street, Kirribilli.'

She wrote it down, astonished at the unwillingness of her hand.

'Right. I'll go there straight away.'

'Thanks. That's a weight off my mind.'

Mr Walter, on his way out, brought the visitor's chair across to her.

'Sit down. I'll get Olive to bring you a cup of tea.' He said respectfully, 'Is it a relative?'

She shook her head, sinking into the chair under the weight of her sadness. She wished she could be the one to comfort Trevor. You built a wall around yourself and too late you found yourself walled in.

Olive came in carrying a cup of tea with two biscuits and a folded paper strip of Aspros in the saucer.

'I have to go. I have to break the news to someone.'

Olive said, 'What a terrible job.' (And what a terrible person to give it to.) 'You're as white as a sheet. You'd better have this first. Take your Aspros. Oh, you'll want a glass of water.'

Mr Walter had thought of that. He came in carrying a glass of water.

He asked, 'Do you know how to get there?'

She shook her head.

'I'll find it for you.' He took his street directory from the bookshelf, found the street and began to draw a map. Who could have imagined such kindness in Mr Walter? 'You can get out at Milson's Point on the right-hand side . . .'

She tried to listen. It did not matter; she would find the street.

Olive said, 'It is a relative?'

She shook her head.

Olive put her arms round her. 'Oh, poor Isobel.'

False pretences, but she put her head against Olive's body and felt the weight of sadness subside a little

'I have to go.'

She began to take account now of what she had to do, and to dread it, remembering what she had done last time she talked to Diana.

Mr Walter handed her the map. 'Don't forget this and don't worry about getting back. We can do without you for the day.'

She mustn't start crying; she wouldn't even be crying about Nick, but because of the sympathy.

She nodded and went. In the outer office the girls watched silently as she covered her typewriter and picked up her bag. She nodded to them too. They didn't want her to speak. How awesome she had become.

Diana, I have bad news, Diana, I've come to tell you . . . Don't say it suddenly. You have to say it somehow. There isn't any way of making it better, remember that, just see to it you don't make it worse. How? Break it gently – here, have a gentle blow over the head.

Her own shock was wearing off and the memory of Nick returning. She could not grieve for him – that would be an intrusion, since she had not really known him – but she grieved enough for beauty gone.

It would be good to be Kenneth and be able to write a poem.

Oh, bugger Kenneth.

She was aghast at the spiteful rage that Kenneth could rouse in her – and at this moment of all moments. Kenneth would write a poem, a beautiful elegy; that would be something left of Nick, and she should be ashamed of herself.

She got out at Milson's Point. Mr Walter's map took her downwards towards the water but stopped half-way in a small street crowded with apartment houses. Number Thirty-four was narrow, dingy white, shabby beside its new-painted tricked-out neighbours. It was dark in the lobby but lighter at the top of the first flight of stairs, where she found Number Seven. She knocked feebly, her stomach sinking away from her, then knocked more firmly.

Inside, a voice called out words of complaint she could not distinguish. There was a pause, then the door was half-opened and Diana looked through the gap.

'Diana, may I come in?.'

Diana opened the door wide. She was wearing a quite dirty nightgown, her hair was tangled and her feet were bare. She stared with puzzled eyes at Isobel.

'Helen asked me to come.'

The bed was unmade, the covers thrown back as if Diana

had just got out of it. On the floor beside it were an unwashed cup, a plate and a greasy knife, an ashtray full of cigarette butts, a paperback open face down, three pairs of shoes lying in disorder – Isobel looked for somewhere to sit, but both the chairs were heaped with clothes.

She's not going to be able to bear it.

Diana, still staring, sat down on the bed.

Isobel hid her face in her hands. What a stagy thing to do, yet she hadn't meant to do it, was surprised that such gestures existed outside books.

It forced Diana to speak, at last.

'What's the matter?'

'Diana, I've got very bad news. Nick is dead.'

She hasn't really heard, sitting there dull-eyed, trying to make out what I said.

'It was an accident, on his bike. I don't know much about it; he was badly hurt and he died this morning in hospital. Helen asked me to come and tell you.'

Absent-mindedly, Diana pulled open the drawer of the bedside table, got out a hairbrush and began to brush her hair.

Shock. People do very funny things when they're shocked. But the feeling that was coming over Diana did not seem like shock. It was profound; she was thinking hard and breathing deeply. She dropped the hairbrush and steadied herself with one hand on the pillow.

This must be what they called being in travail. It was a private process; Isobel should go away and let her get on with it, but she did not know how to do that.

The feeling was appearing now: relief. Isobel was the prison governor who had brought her news of her reprieve.

She said, 'Can I get you something? Make you a cup of tea?'

What falsehood. I am thinking of what she ought to be feeling.

Diana too thought Isobel had made a social error.

'No, thank you. I'm quite all right.'

She looked with surprise at the hairbrush and put it back in the drawer.

All right is no word for it. She's glad he's dead. She feels the way I felt when my mother died. He wasn't a human being to her, he was a thorn in her side, a stone in her shoe.

What price love, then?

She ought to pretend. She ought to have the decency to pretend, after all she's said and done.

'Nick's mother is at the hospital. She's coming to the house to collect his things. Helen said, if you'd mind not coming here just for the moment, you know . . . it's going to be very difficult, with Nick's mother there.'

Diana said, in a sharp irritable tone, 'Why would I want to go there?'

Now she was looking round the room, looking as if she had just woken up and was wondering at the mess.

She got up. 'Thank you for coming to tell me.' Quite the social tone. 'Tell Helen I'm very sorry, won't you? It's very tragic. There isn't much one can say, is there?'

Isobel was looking for an exit line, but she did not need one, for Diana was ushering her towards the door.

She was more depressed now than grieved. Walking back to the station, she remembered Auden:

'I've come a very long way to prove
No land, no water and no love.'

How could she know? Grief might visit Diana later. After all, what did it matter to her whether or not Diana grieved for Nick? It did matter very much, though she did not know why.

Now she had to go to Fifty-one. She did not want to;

she was fighting off the shameful thought that grief was a terrible bore. Perhaps it wasn't such a shameful thought – grief might be like that, being slammed into a lockup with one thought you couldn't get away from. She wouldn't be able to get away from it even if she did stay away from Fifty-one.

Helen opened the door to her and said, out of a pinched white face, 'Am I glad to see you, I was going mad here by myself. Dan's away on a trip and Trevor went to the University. He had a tutorial, he thought he'd better do it, he hadn't had time to call it off. Anyhow, he's probably better doing something. They've been friends since school, you know.' Talking steadily, she had led Isobel into the kitchen. 'Would you like a cup of coffee? Did you go to see Diana? How did she take it?'

'Better than you would expect. She didn't react much at all, really.'

'She probably hasn't taken it in, yet. I don't think I have. Did you explain about not coming here?'

'Yes. She seemed surprised that I'd think she would.'

'I hope we haven't put the idea into her head.'

Diana would be down at the laundry with her dirty washing, or cleaning up her room, or looking in Positions Vacant. Don't let's worry about Diana.

They carried their coffee into the living room. Isobel would have liked something to eat but felt she could not mention hunger.

'The motorist just didn't see the bike, apparently. I don't know whether Nick was speeding – he did sometimes. It seemed like a bit of a joke.'

Outside, a car stopped, a car door thudded shut. Helen looked alarmed.

'Oh, my God, is it . . . I thought they were going to keep her at the hospital for the day.'

The knocker sounded. Helen got up and went to the

door, coming back full of politeness and dread, ushering a small, neat, fair-haired woman with a thin handsome face, not at all like Nick. The woman was staring in front of her with isolated eyes.

Helen said, 'We would have come to get you. I'm sorry you had to come alone.'

'It's quite all right.' The tone of her voice didn't match the look on her face; it would have done for a more social occasion. 'There's so much to be done, you see. I want to get his things packed and catch the night train.'

'But Mrs Drummond . . .' Helen looked at her, baffled. 'Have you had lunch? Can I get you something to eat?'

'No, thank you. I had something at the hospital. Where . . .?'

She stood looking about the living room, looking for a door.

If Helen tries to stop her, she will go quite mad. Isobel looked at Helen, who had perhaps reached the same conclusion.

'Upstairs,' said Helen. 'I'll show you.'

'Thank you very much, but I'd rather go by myself. You do understand?'

She sounded quite social.

'Yes, of course. At the top of the stairs, first on the left.'

When she had gone, Helen said, 'I suppose it's better for her to have something to do. But that stony calm. If only we could do something for her.'

'What could anyone do?'

They sat, cowed by the silence upstairs. Then the voice started. It sounded thin, wailed without words, then said, 'No . . . no, no, no.' Each time louder and more frantic. 'No!' Then it was word and scream together, then a scream without words. Then silence. She began again, almost reasonably, 'No, no.'

Helen had her hands over her ears. She said angrily, 'She

shouldn't have come alone. She ought to have somebody with her.'

Isobel was thinking, 'Who would ever risk this?'

The noise had sunk and grown again. It wasn't something to hear any more, but something to see, the words like flung stones, the screams like wheeling bird-flight.

Helen made for the stairs and Isobel followed.

She was sitting on the bed, mouth stretched in a scream, holding a jacket she must have been folding when despair interrupted.

Helen began, 'Mrs Drummond,' but stopped because she was out of reach.

'Did they give you anything to take at the hospital?'

She knew they were there but she wasn't going to admit it.

Her handbag was on the chest of drawers. Isobel opened it, feeling guilt and pity because opening the poor woman's handbag without permission was like treating her as a drunk or an idiot, and found a round white plastic box with a label: MRS DRUMMOND TWO EVERY FOUR HOURS. She gave the box to Helen and went down to the kitchen for a glass of water. How glad she was to get out of the room, how reluctant to go back.

Clinging to the jacket still, Mrs Drummond seemed to be all obstinate denial, but she took the tablets without protest, giving up her revolt against fate.

'Into Trevor's room,' Helen murmured. 'You must come and rest, you can't go back tonight. I'll ring the farm for you, just come and lie down.'

Together they urged her into Trevor's room, took the jacket out of her hands but left it on the bed, close to her, took off her shoes, pulled down the blind to shut out the useless day.

She lay still, waiting for them to leave her. They went out quietly, as if she was sleeping.

Downstairs, Helen said, 'Stay a bit, do you mind? Trevor ought to be back soon.'

She had not thought of seeing Trevor again, would have expected to be overcome with shame if she met him by chance, but that scene was insignificant now.

'I wonder if I should get a doctor for her. I don't know. I'll wait and see how the tablets work, I think.'

Helen spoke languidly, expecting no answer. Then they sat listening nervously to the silence.

Trevor came in with the grimace of age on his face and nodded to Isobel from the other side of the river. Helen went to him, put her arms round him and her head on his shoulder. He put his cheek against hers and they stood quietly together.

Isobel went away. She did not belong with them, though they had not shut her out.

She walked back to the house where she had seen the sign ROOM VACANT.

When she came into the dining room that night she talked to the kitchen door and said, 'Mrs Bowers, I'll be leaving at the end of the week.'

In the kitchen Mrs Bowers spoke to Mrs Prendergast, a mumble that sounded like 'Good riddance.'

Isobel came to the table with tears running down her face, so that Betty said with compunction, 'Don't let her get you down.'

Isobel shook her head. 'It isn't that.'

You could change your name, have your face altered, change your country and your language, but in the end you would resurrect your self.

Nevertheless, she felt cheerful as she packed her belongings. She was glad to be escaping from a grief not her own, she looked forward to the foolish pleasure of buying a saucepan and a frying pan, a cup and saucer and

a plate, a knife, a fork and a spoon and two tea towels.
Into the suitcase she put Shakespeare, Keats, Byron (now
known as facile), Shelley, Auden. Though she knew the
passage of Auden well, she found the place and read it
with a grin.

'It's no use turning nasty,
It's no use turning good.
You're what you are and nothing you do
Will get you out of the wood.'

She shut the book and put it in the suitcase.
One is never quite alone.

5 · I For Isobel

Isobel woke up out of a blue and gold dream: a sheltered bay, shining water, little boats drifting like thoughts.

She was staring at a strange ceiling. She shut her eyes and tried to snuggle back into the dream but it was too late; it had dwindled to its source, the breath of the young man asleep beside her as it beat, soft and warm, on her shoulder.

Eyes open, back to the ceiling: ornate plaster, baskets of flowers linked by swags of ribbon, a stain in one corner, yellow, like ... sunshine? butter? honey? paler than pumpkin, darker than pee. Dirty old daylight, if there was a word.

There are words. Words we have plenty of, nasty little buzzing insects that they are. Awake two minutes and the word factory is at it already. And you at the loom, zoom, zoom.

It was going to be a bad day.

It's a stain-coloured stain and shut up.

The stain advanced like a finger on the soured white plaster. In the corner a clotted cobweb softer than dust. Like Miss Havisham's wedding cake.

She would have to expect a bad day, after last night.

Thrown out, from Kate's place. Told to bugger off and not come back.

Well, you were always wondering whether you'd go to Kate's place or not – that's one question settled. But thrown out! Ouch!

Don't try to laugh it off, it was ouch! all right, walking that long mile to the door with knees unhinged and each foot weighing a ton.

Just the same, that story Fred was telling was repulsive. Like a long cold snake it slid meandering through an underground littered with the private rubbish of the human body. That was the sentence she had been working on last night, to keep her mind off the story, so her grin must have slipped and that had given Kate the chance to pounce. But she must have been waiting to pounce, beforehand, to pick a thing like that. OK, she was at the bellicose stage but there were other people who were listening with fixed grins, out of politeness.

Politeness cropped up in some funny places.

Not with Kate, though.

'Who the hell do you think you are, sitting there with that superior look on your face? If you don't like what you hear at my place get out, go on, bugger off and don't come back. You only come here anyhow to see what you can pick up.'

The hideous speech rang in her head again and she thought a hardy ouch! to drown a whimper.

Superior. If they only knew!

The funny thing was that Kate didn't seem to think much of the story either, and by the third paragraph Fred was sounding strained and needed rescue. As for picking people up – that was why quite a few people went to Kate's, but Isobel knew that what was tolerated in other people was not forgiven in her. She very much wished to know why this was so.

The remark about picking people up must have sent this Michael after her, to wander about the streets, the conversation wandering too, inconclusive, till he said, impatient as if that was what they had been talking about and for too long, 'Well, are you coming back to my place or aren't you?' You couldn't blame him for being casual, 'no' being the word it was, but still . . . O lyric love, half angel and half bird, or ninety-nine per cent bird.

She turned her head to look at him, remote in sleep: delicate sallow oblong face, fluted upper lip, light-brown crimped hair drifting across his forehead . . . Listen, you don't have to paint his portrait.

Doctor, I have this problem. Some people count lamp posts, I describe them. You don't think that's a problem? You should try it sometimes, like five lamp posts one after the other, a word picture of each, to be handed in nowhere at the end of the day . . .

She changed position carefully, not wanting the young man to wake. When they woke, you had to start guessing, how to look, what to say, what they wanted you to be. Always guessing wrong.

There was the young man who had said, 'Why can't you be yourself a little more?'

That got right under your skin and it's still there like a splinter, because what to answer?

I am the vacuum Nature abhors. And not only Nature, come to that.

Kate was drunk. Don't worry about Kate.

That's when the truth comes out.

What to answer?

Nobody home.

She had bent to look at the child in the stroller, had started back from the white triangular idiot face sagging against the canvas. The stout nursewoman wheeling it had tapped her forehead and murmured, 'Nobody home.'

That was Isobel's story, if she knew where to tap. Not the head. Plenty going on there, the word factory spinning and spinning and what for? Thoughts running like mice on a treadmill and a door held straining against memories . . .

She bolted out of the bed, made for the bathroom and sat on the loo, staring at a different ceiling, this time as narrow as a corridor and slightly concave . . .

Panic. There she was, exposed to the public, peeing, naked, her clothes far out of reach – a horror dream, in daylight.

She laughed. It was the ceiling. Something about the ceiling, size, shape and colour, had set her up in a train compartment. There was a mind for you, darting about on its own adventures, giving the owner the fright of a lifetime. Lucky you got a laugh out of it now and then.

She washed her smiling face in cold water, wiped it on the edge of a dank towel and went back to the bedroom.

There was a bookcase against the wall by the door. She knelt in front of it: *Portrait of the Artist as a Young Man*, *An American Tragedy*, *The Oxford Book of English Verse*, *Pylon*, *Sanctuary*, Penguins, colour-cued to the young man's interests, drawing a map of his mind's country, where she wished, fleetingly, she could meet him. Not much chance of that.

From the bed he said, 'I wouldn't have taken you for a bookish type.'

His cool, inexpressive voice made her think with regret of the blue and gold dream. Her voice came jovial and too loud.

'You can't tell me by my cover either, you see.'

'And – just – what – cover – would – that – be?'

Oh, hell. Rich with contained amusement, the voice. And the pauses even more so.

She heard herself say with mad politeness, 'Do you like

Faulkner? I've only read *Light in August*. I was most impressed.'

Graciously. If anything could make it worse. Like putting a hat on. More naked than ever, she plunged for cover into a book. Four inches by six, dizzying disparity, but old and shabby, therefore her own. She sat staring at a page, not reading. He might have a thing about nakedness – she had a thing about it herself now that she knew what it was. Adam and Eve weren't in it. She must have been thinking about fig leaves, grabbing a book that size.

He had put out the light last night before they had undressed. She had thought it funny, groping about in the dark for the chair to put her clothes on.

'Now I wonder,' he said vaguely, not wondering, 'about girls like you. I wonder why you do things like this.'

What does he mean 'things like this'? There's only one thing like this.

That's the question, though. The one with the hundred inadequate answers.

There's the connection with love – the dubious connection.

You do it because you can. Two ways to do it and our Isobel would get it wrong.

You like to join the human race on the only level you can manage.

There is a deeper reason, but it has no words. It is a landscape, an unlighted desert strewn with epic lumber, dead machines, stopped clocks. All my own work. Call it INERTIA.

Wouldn't he gape if you said it was a religious rite – perform it often enough and the god might descend.

'I might wonder why you do things like this. But I don't think I would have asked.'

Who said that?

You did, and in a tone you didn't know you could use, detached and easy.

It was the book. There was no doubt about it, the calm she felt flowed into her from the solid little faded book in her hand. She read the title, *Words of the Saints*. Mysterious.

A feeling of freedom, of stepping out of chains.

He said, 'It doesn't mean much to you physically, that's obvious.'

Oh. He had caught on to that. Even on that level, you can't really join the human race.

She said, 'Is that a real question? I mean, do you want to know the answer?'

'I would hardly have asked if I didn't.' But he sounded shaken, defensive.

'You might have wanted me to know that you disapproved of me.'

The bedsprings squawked. To be accused of disapproval was a keen thrust.

You're not yourself, Isobel. You're somebody a whole lot smarter.

And that was a reason for leaving him alone; if she was smarter than he was, she could afford to.

He wanted her out before he got up. Knobbly knees. Her legs remembered them like sharp enormous knuckles inside her own. It was a bit sad, really, the approach that was half joke and half quarrel, then working and moaning and gasping together in the dark (and one of them putting on an act, at that), avoiding all signs of love, and what they had in common, the map of the mind and dislike of their bodies, not to be spoken of.

Meanwhile, she was testing the mysterious quality of the book. She put it down, panic threatened. She picked it up and was calm.

Amazing. I wave this wand.

Well, she had to go and get her clothes from that chair on the other side of the bed and she couldn't take it with her. What a traverse! But if she didn't move they would be found there, two corpses dead of starvation, one in a bed and the other in front of a bookcase.

She memorised the book: purple cloth fading to a dead leaf brown, paper like dirty old daylight, like the ceiling stain . . . a little devil thought popped into her head, of teasing him into being really nasty. That would make it so much easier to steal the book.

How her mind reacted to that one, all of a piece, was astounding: like a rabble finding formation to present a firm capital NO like the Harp of Erin on Saint Patrick's Day. Freedom, indeed – she felt as if she had walked into a fence.

A safety fence.

She was going to steal the book, just the same. She slid it into place on the shelf, stood bravely up and walked, without straightening her shoulders or pulling her stomach in (she had her pride) to the chair where her clothes were.

After all, he shut his eyes, so it was no ordeal. That was polite of him – she was sorry she was going to steal his book. Quickly she put on bra and briefs, blouse and skirt, found her comb in her bag and, combing her hair, said, 'Shall I make a cup of coffee? Would you like one?'

Frail and pained, he murmured with closed eyes, 'Not for me, thank you.' Then his eyes opened, seeing release. 'But make one, if you'd like one. You'll find the stuff in the cupboard over the sink.'

'Thanks.'

She stepped into her sandals, picked up her bag and left it in front of the bookcase (cunning, cunning), and went into the kitchen. Sure enough, while she was looking for the coffee in the cupboard she heard the bathroom door shut. She listened; the cistern roared. When she heard the shower running, she sped into the bedroom, took the book and put it in her bag, loosened books to hide the space, opened the door that led to the stairs and the street and shut it quietly behind her.

She ran down the stairs and opened the front door on to bright daylight in an empty street lined with houses still sleeping, closed on a secret life like the book. That was good, life presenting a mystery. Made it seem alive.

That's a brilliant thought, Isobel, making life seem alive. Well, she knew what she meant, if thousands wouldn't.

That was the kind of thought that set the word factory groaning, grinding and defining, but for once the word factory was out of action, and oh! the peace and quiet.

She stepped out happily until she turned the corner into a broad quiet street of trees and handsome houses that led to a main road where cars were flashing past already. On the far corner, a telephone box.

Memory rose like vomit. Now you remember who you are, Isobel. You're a pervert, a phone freak.

But not any more, not any more. Does time ever pass?

Not for you. For you time never passes. Time becomes space in your mind.

Crimson, pagoda-roofed, the phone box leered like an evil little joss house for one devil worshipper. She forced herself towards it, thinking angrily, 'What made them listen? Why didn't they put the phone down straight away?' Well, some of them had, and that had become part of the game, fishing up a victim on the end of her invisible line – and in the end there was always a listener, a puzzled voice giving the cues she wanted, not able to free itself in time.

Collecting pennies for the phone had been a dirty private pleasure but the best worst moment had been when the words came, and she shuddered with satisfaction as she let out the stream of hatred. The kind of bang other people must get out of sex.

She bent in misery, remembering the calm scornful voice that had said without pity, 'What an unhappy person you must be.' She had put the phone down, writhing in defeat and humiliation, had plunged out of the box . . . she was writhing now, the pain as bad as ever . . . she felt in her bag, seized the book, held it against her chest.

Christ but it was comic (though far from funny) standing there in the street pointing bone against bone, book against telephone box, but it worked. She straightened up and walked towards the box, in control. And why not? If a telephone box can make you sick to your stomach, why shouldn't a book make you feel better? Coming close to the box, with the book held up solemnly in front of her – she couldn't help guying the situation, it was so fantastic – she felt a needle-thrust of sorrow, remembering the one voice that had answered her with a cry of sadness. That was the one that had stopped her with a real answer; crying 'I'm sorry, I'm sorry,' she had put the phone down on the dirty little game for ever. Like in a black fairytale, the formula had turned toad – well, not into prince, don't get carried away – but into a human being of sorts. I wish she could know what she did for me, she thought. Perhaps she did know; perhaps the cry 'I'm sorry' had carried its message.

She was past the phone box. Round the corner there was a bus stop and a city-bound bus was coming. She ran to board it, walked past a few passengers, numb-faced with sleep or boredom, to the back of the bus, sat with the book on her knee, thinking, 'Readable, too,' – which was as funny as if it had been edible. It fell open at a page – she liked that, a sort of ghost-communication – but oh, hell, it was St John of the Cross, not a fun character at all. No joy in the yellowed page, the mean tiny print and St John of the Cross on self and senses: *The soul must of necessity – if we would attain to the Divine union of God – pass through the obscure night of mortification of*

the desires, and self-denial in all things. The reason is that
all the love we bestow on creatures is in the eyes of God
mere darkness, and that while we are involved therein, the
soul is incapable of being enlightened and possessed by
the pure and simple light of God, unless we first cast it
away.

Therein – what a fat, complacent word.

She shut the book, wishing she had one or two of the
things the saints had cast away. Wouldn't even mind a
few desires.

Well, that was a washout.

Once it was shut, the book was a talisman again.
Mysterious. Book against telephone box – she knew what
the telephone box meant all right, but what was it about
the book? The cover? A faded purple cushion? Happiness
in a room with purple curtains? In Auntie Ann's house?
Purple wasn't in, then. Purple was religion and funerals.
If you did know, the charm might stop working. Take what
comes and be thankful.

She got off the bus at Central, walked up to the station
to get a cup of coffee in the cafeteria, then to the Ladies.
She had put the book on the ledge above the basin and
was doing her hair, looking in the glass and hating her
face, as usual, because she had got so much of it from her
mother: little mouth with thick full-blown lips, sharp chin
and heavy straight eyebrows, a face made for gloom, people
always telling her she was sulking when she wasn't, when
the face shaped and softened with the beginning of a laugh
because she was thinking those features weren't her
mother's; she had had the tenancy of them for fifty years
but they had been on the go for generations; that nose had
taken snuff, sniffed at pomanders, plague posies, smelling
salts, rose hip, orris root – things she had never smelt and
never would – as well as honeysuckle, gas leaks and
lavender, not to mention . . . and the mouth had prayed

and cursed, kissed and said 'I love you' – it must have, to get so far, it stood to reason . . . and the eyes – what cities had they seen? What arches, branches, long galleries of leaves becalmed, sober asphalt leading down to drunken sad-breathed seas, spires pointing out of the dirty brocade that sunlight lays on house-covered slopes . . .

She loved the place, the world, the vast, the multitudinous . . . blue-white pinnacles, marble mirrored in still water, lost cities overgrown, mysterious altars, forests and castles and the great shining slow-moving glaciers, the infinity of skylines . . . the wealth of the world and the sense of being nineteen years old, those cells fruiting so precisely into eyes and mouth and all, every one of them nineteen years old, sent her upwards on a Ferris wheel of joy, so that she bent her head forward to hide her shining face behind the fall of hair she was combing till she settled quietly on earth again.

She was still so carried away though that she went without the book, ran back to get it and put it in her bag with such relief – shabby little object that it was – she had to laugh at herself.

And speaking of books . . . *My Book of Picture Stamps of the World* – India: The Taj Mahal; Peru (Cuzco): The Ancient Temple of the Sun; A Peasant of the Pyrenees . . . it was out of those sober little stamps that the great wheeling vision of the world had come. How strange, a joy you cellared when you were maybe ten years old coming up so drinkable at nineteen.

Feeling buoyant enough to go back and face her room, instead of drifting about the town, she took a bus to Glebe and walked to the rooming house. Buoyancy was needed when she opened the door on the squalor of the room, the unwashed china and the greasy frying pan on the table, the heap of dirty clothes on the floor in the corner – a person couldn't make such a mess by accident, she must have been trying to tell herself something.

Silence and solitude. Silence had started the word factory, solitude had driven her to the evil telephone game. Squalor within demanded squalor without: she dropped her dirty clothes in the corner and was more depressed to see them there.

One works from the laundry bag inwards. Suiting action to thought, she took the bag from the hook behind the door and put the clothes in it.

She didn't have to be solitary. She could go with Frank to Party meetings, where, he said, she would meet people like herself.

'I don't try to sell it to people usually, Isobel. I just happen to think it's the right thing for you.'

'You have to think what they tell you to think.'

'But what they tell you is right.'

She wanted a cause to live for but could not adopt one; the cause would have to find her.

Sitting on the bed, she looked around her, considering how to make the room more liveable. The worst thing in sight, apart from the dirty dishes, now that she had (so easily!) removed the heap of clothes, was the flap of wallpaper hanging loose above the table. She had tried to glue it once; the glue had failed and she had resigned herself to it, though it nagged at her with the urge to seize it and rip, making things worse. She could trim that off and hide the patch, tack up a colour print from a magazine – she was caught by a longing for richness, for padded satin stitch glowing in crimson and russet, a panel of embroidery.

You could make one.

Of the dogs of the past that were always yapping at her heels, one nipped her so that she winced. Well known for her exquisite embroidery, our Isobel. Miss Harman the sewing teacher. Bitch. 'Now bring out your work, Isobel

Callaghan.' (Free design for a flower in long and short stitch, or filled-in stem, choose your colours from the cotton box, girls.) Out she had bustled, expecting praise (Miss Harman's tone having promised the class a treat) for the big shining flower with streaks of pink and scarlet radiating from its crimson centre. Not warned by all the others with their demure roses shading from pink to cream, their yellow-eyed white daisies.

'And what kind of flower is this, Isobel?' Miss Harman's lips had twitched. 'Is it a rose? Do you think it is a rose, girls?' She had held it up for the class to see (as Isobel had foreseen, but so differently). 'No, I don't think it's a rose.' The class had begun to snigger, perceiving that it was invited to a moment's holiday. 'I don't believe I've ever seen a flower like that, and I'm sure I would have remembered.'

Shouts of laughter and Isobel not knowing what to do with the smile on her face. She had to get rid of it as best she could, knowing that its slow fading would be the best part of the joke, so she widened it and pretended to go along with the laughter. That had made Miss Harman furious. She had handed back the piece of cloth saying, 'Go back to your place, you stupid girl. There is nothing funny about vulgar bad taste.'

Saint John of the Cross was right up the pole. The obscure night of mortification of the desires and self-denial in all things – what came of that was people like Miss Harman. Saints that get drafted. Compulsory sainthood.

Well, she had put Isobel off embroidery for life.

But why? She still felt in her fingers the pleasure of placing the silk thread deftly and precisely. Miss Harman was far away, perhaps dead, and Isobel could embroider flowers in any colour she liked, pink, purple, whatever. This was known as freedom. She began to laugh, then looked at the clock. Ten to eleven; she could make it to

Grace Brothers and shop before closing time. She jumped up, ran to the loo and back, picked up her bag and was off again, crazy for the embroidery panel.

She came back gasping with fatigue after a rush of shopping and dropped her parcels on the bed: a book of embroidery designs, carbon paper, tracing paper, pencil, ruler, scissors and needles, linen, silks (no purple after all – bronze, gold, crimson, cream, pink, olive green, dead-leaf brown). She opened the book of designs to the one she had chosen, a stylised tree bearing an improbable miscellany of flowers, fruit and birds.

How much she had to do before the desired moment when she would thread her needle and set the first stitch: trace the design, enlarge the tracing, trace the enlargement onto the linen. Also wash up, eat, wash up, find out what the book meant . . .

Working on the tracing went well with pondering.

One thought she had been dodging – suppose it was religion that gave the book its power? If it was, too bad. Religion was out. She used to think a lot about God; then, one day, she had asked herself if He existed, and that had been that. But she had had a religious craze once – she must have been quite small, for the plaster feet with their painted blood and the ghastly nail driven through them were at eye level when she had knelt in front of the big crucifix. It had been kid stuff – God the imaginary friend – going in to pray, or to visit, before she went home (one might well). She had given it up quite soon because as an imaginary friend God was limited. You couldn't tell Him everything, you had to be on your best behaviour. Besides, she hadn't liked Him, and the more she had dealt with Him, the less she had liked Him. No, it couldn't be religion. What the book meant, the atmosphere . . . aura . . . shut up, this is important . . . the book meant friendship, company at least. Communication and understanding.

If she had ever had that, she wanted to know it. Boring or not, the book had to be tackled.

When she grew tired of tracing, she went back to the book and considered opening it.

Come on, it isn't all Saint John of the Cross. Some of the saints were real dashers, like Augustine (not yet!) and Saint Thomas More.

How did she know? Something stirred in the dead country. How did she know so much about the saints? Not from the convent; she had left it too young – and there it was all bright little holy pictures of the nuns' favourites. Saint Joan in silvery armour had been Isobel's favourite, Saint Isabel being a dull old queen who didn't rate holy pictures and Saint Agnes with her lamb, her eyes turned towards Heaven, altogether too much of the good child. Those holy pictures were a bright spot in memory; there were special ones, set on plaster of paris with a ribbon to hang them by, prizes for good work – she could remember carrying one home, full of pride at having done the right thing for once.

The book.

She tried Augustine first, thinking of that prayer: Give me chastity and . . . something . . . only not yet. It wasn't there, surprise, surprise. They had the scene in the garden, but she skipped that because it made her nervous, the thought of being tapped on the shoulder, press-ganged, by the Almighty or anything else.

Saint John of the Cross. Now come on, no dodging.

She read the instructions for entering the dark night of the senses, trying to give them respectful attention though she thought that anyone who gave away worldly pleasures when he didn't have to was mad.

Rules for mortifying truly the desire for honour . . . well, here's something for you, Isobel.

1. *Do those things which bring thee into contempt, and*

desire that others may do them. (Like wearing a notice
KICK ME on the appropriate spot. You do that all
right.)

*2. Speak disparagingly of thyself, and contrive that others
may do so too.* (You're still in.)

*3. Think humbly and contemptuously of thyself, and
contrive that others may do so also.*

It was such a picture of Isobel the nuisance that she had
begun to giggle at the first one and after the third she was
laughing quietly but steadily. Well, well; on the way to
Heaven and she hadn't known it.

Still grinning, she turned to Saint Thomas More.

On Death

*. . . Reckon me now yourself a young man in your best
lust, twenty years of age, if ye will. Let there be another
ninety. Both must ye die, both be ye in the cart carrying
forward. His gallows and death standeth within ten miles
of the farthest, and yours within eighty. I see not why ye
should reckon much less of your death than he, though
your way may be longer, since ye shall never cease riding
till ye come at it.*

That had wiped the grin off her face. Her tears indeed
had begun to run quietly as she read *young man in your
best lust.* They were for Nick, for whom she hadn't felt
entitled to grieve – but she was entitled; she was one of
them. She saw Helen and Trevor, holding each other so
tenderly, but Mr Walter, too, and Olive, moved to such
kindness as they heard the rumble of the cart.

She closed the book. It wasn't news, of course. Mrs
Prendergast had had the same message, but Saint Thomas
More put it better. It was just the putting it better that
made it news.

Mortality. That's where love and brotherhood have to
start, in what we have in common: you belong because
you are mortal. Like: *Never send to know for whom*

the bell tolls – that isn't religion, it's a kind of poetry.

And for those who hear nothing, the dead in life, her mother and Diana – you could shed a tear for them, too, but don't get carried away. Look to your own awakening.

That was enough of the book for today. She went back to her tracing, knowing what she had to do tomorrow. She must go back to the suburb she grew up in, retracing her steps to see if she could find a memory, a clue to the meaning of the book. She could hardly believe it of herself that she was going down memory lane, can you imagine, what a scenic tour, the corner where she had wet her pants and waddled home with the cold wet cloth sagging between her legs and Deirdre Fitzgerald following her all the way uttering complicated peals of grown-up laughter and pointing to her wet socks.

That memory encouraged her, because she didn't feel any particular shame at seeing it again, could have been either of the little girls, the one waddling or the one laughing; you had so little choice in what you did.

Now she put two and two together and connected the agonies of her bladder with the big girl, the class dunce with the moomoo eyes and the long, spindly legs, who had defended the entrance to the lavatories against her, dodging from side to side with hands outstretched ready to slap. Jesus Christ, everybody has the right to go to the lavatory; you don't have to be a charmer for that. She looked back at the waddling figure with a new tolerance.

She woke up next morning knowing at once what she had to do, but putting the thought of it away for the moment. She spent the morning washing her clothes and working on the enlargement – at this rate she would put in the first stitch this weekend. The loose flap would still be visible, of course – she was amused at that, but it did not matter, since she had discovered a small authentic piece of her lost self.

After lunch, she got ready to go out. One thing, it wasn't far to go. As she went to the bathroom, she thought, the bathroom being at the back of the house, this is the furthest point, and the loo being at the back of the bathroom . . . what a thought. At least there wasn't anybody dancing about in front of it, that was progress. But how far? Two miles? Not very far to travel in nineteen years, not counting work, of course, and some excursions, like that boarding house where they used to spend the summer holidays, but that was different – she had been taken there. On her own, she hadn't got far.

She put the book in her bag, the charm against phone boxes and who knew what else.

It mightn't be as bad as she expected.

The funny thing was, she reflected on her way to the bus stop, the funny thing was that, though it was a short journey in space, it seemed like a long one, in time, yet she had left less than a year ago. It couldn't be a year since Margaret had stood crying in the empty lounge room, while Isobel stood breathing the air of freedom.

The suburb she was going to visit belonged to earlier days. She had a confused thought about the city one builds, the insect city with its threadlike paths, inside the geographical maps.

In the street there were couples strolling, following their own ant-tracks. One couple had stopped to look in a shop window; in the halted stroller the woman had been wheeling, a silk-skinned jewel-eyed baby had captured one of its swivelling legs, thrust the foot, covered with a lacy white sock, into its mouth and was sucking it steadily.

In the cart carrying forward. Not strollers, she thought with horror, hearing remembered screams, thinking what the price of human love might be.

When she got into the bus, she was still thinking with anxiety of the enchanting, perishable baby. The cart carrying forward was not a thought to dwell on. Do not dwell on the thought that we dwell in the cart. She squashed the little insect word as it came to life, before it could distract her. This is serious; you are mortal but you must live as if you were immortal – otherwise, who would dare?

Love begins in the mortal flesh and must not know it.

You'd be like Mrs Prendergast, making offerings to the idol every minute, sighs and lovely wreaths and little white coffins . . . forget it. It was bad enough, thinking of that baby growing into, dying into, a stout woman with varicose veins and a hairy wart on her chin – that was death at the rate one could stand it.

One must know and not know. It was evident that there were degrees of knowing. Or else think so much of life, to believe it was worth it. Worth the coming and the going.

The bus stopped at the top of the main street of her home suburb. She got off and walked. How quiet it was! Parramatta Road had drawn off all the Sunday walkers; the street was empty, and not only of people. Of course, this stretch, from the church to Parramatta Road, had never been one of her ant-tracks.

She looked about like a tourist at the old-fashioned houses, the fanlights, stained-glass panels like Fifty-one's, steps with marble treads and patterned tiles set in the . . . what was it called, the vertical face? There was a special word . . .

Then it began. All the nameless things threatened and the colours pestered: sea-jade, chocolate, no word for the sullen grey-flaked white of marble.

She felt for the book, took hold and the word factory stood still. She walked on, protected.

Here was the church, in red brick crumbling away at the corners, so inoffensive . . . why hadn't she gone in, attended Mass and thought her own thoughts? Plenty of other people did, no doubt, but not our Isobel. She had to skulk about back streets, pretending she was going to ten o'clock, walking, walking, rapt in a mutter of thoughts she was too frightened to express, like, I have a right to my beliefs, as much as anybody else, but petrified all the time with the fear of being seen and reported to her mother.

She felt guilty still, not of missing Mass, but of the skulking and the fear, but no more guilty here than elsewhere, less perhaps, because the old building made a statement of peaceful indifference.

As she walked through the dim porch, with its rack of pamphlets and its parish notices, the holy-water stoup made no claim, but when she went into the church, she understood why she couldn't have treated it with contempt, a church having it over other buildings, in that it was always a shell, so much less important than what filled it – at this moment, shadowy peace and quiet, stained, here and there, by patches of wordless emotion. Around the big crucifix at the back, she sensed not prayer, but a faded anguish; the crucifix was smaller than it used to be, which was right for the scenes of childhood: the blood-marked feet which had loomed at eye level were now of neat size and remarkably close to the floor. The church broke the rules, being bigger than she remembered.

About the confessional hovered guilt and unease. At each side of the altar a kneeling angel held the stem of a bright brass candelabrum which branched and sprouted candlesticks, each one tipped with a tiny whitish bulb like a deformed fingernail – she had pinned some furious analogies to those bulbs, glaring secretly from behind her prayer book, condemning artificial virtue, artificial candlelight, artificial devotion, and they were still there, maybe prompting other young anarchists to meditation. There must be a gentlemanly salesman with a hypnotic smile and a slight limp behind the counter at Pellegrini's. 'I recommend these, Father. They are very . . . attractive.'

You'll go to Hell, Isobel Callaghan, for laughing in church.

The pulpit was a surprise. She could have sworn it was higher and enclosed in carved oak, but it was low-set, unpretentious, with only a faded red curtain hanging from a brass rail. The pulpit for some reason touched her feelings, giving out the same friendly calm as the book.

God, you're a nut, going about like a water diviner holding a twig in front of you waiting for it to dip . . . yet she had felt it twitch in her hand and was disturbed.

She stood waiting, but the pulpit had nothing to say to her, so she went out walking along past the presbytery to the school and a memory she didn't have to grope for, the terrible day of the mental arithmetic test. Fifty questions and Isobel has got them all right, so she is sitting alone among empty desks, the rest of the class being crowded round the walls. There is to be one more question each and the wrong answer will bring down the cane the nun is brandishing. One thin little girl with bright straight brass-coloured hair has grey eyes that hold a skyful of fear. Isobel's face is expressionless. Nobody else knows what that word means; it is not being calm like marble, but naked, skinless. It is a disgusting failure of privacy, like an exposed liver.

Why couldn't you have got a couple wrong? Why did you have to set such a standard for the rest of them? But how many would be safe? You might have been out there too, and you couldn't risk that, could you?

She peered through the wire fence, past the camphor laurel trees, at the neat pale concrete of the playground, empty of children and of ghosts. No ghost running – she had walked, first, with the others gathering behind her, keeping stamping time with her tread, and whether she quickened her step or they did, she did not know, but she was running, round the side of the building to the cul-de-sac of the lavatories – poor thinking, Isobel, but then, what's the use of thinking? That won't help you. She had run, with the pack after her, and had fetched up in an angle between the brick buttress and the wall. She had turned round in despair and had found the leading boy close behind her, so close that their eyes had met uncomfortably. And after all, nothing. Nothing had happened. The boy had advanced his hand, given her hair a gentle, ceremonial tweak, then stood staring. Somebody at the back had shouted, 'Get on with it,' and so released him to turn and shout, 'Mind your own fucking business,' and to plunge back into the mob which rolled away on its new centre. Leaving her disappointed. She had not been so close to anyone before.

She followed the fence around the corner, found the buttress of brick and the sloping half-brick which covered the join between the thicker base and the upper part – stopped and gaped, because she remembered the purplish sloping half-brick coming level with her nose. The mental arithmetic expert, the political animal, the survivor, was a little girl twelve-and-a-half bricks high.

Isobel Callaghan, pick on somebody your own size.

Another thing that astonished about the bricks was their nakedness: no Isobel there, hiding her guilty face in the angle, nothing but a piece of information, a true memory. Of course, in a true memory, you don't see yourself. All the miserable self-images were invention, or at least embroidery.

She hoped nobody would ever find out what a fool she was.

As she walked back past the the church another memory popped up and made her halt, seeing a young priest standing in the pulpit, looking with a friendly face at the congregation, talking about insects that scuttled in the cobwebbed cell of the soul, looking right into Isobel and accepting what he saw.

And that was it. It all came now, the calm elation, the sense of everything solved, of peace.

She had received the Holy Ghost, or something.

Well, she had known from the beginning that it was a mistake, meant for the woman next to her, probably. Just the same, having found herself in a state of grace, she had done her best to keep it, and managed it for a few weeks. She understood the saints and their eccentricities, like sitting on poles and not washing, because the joy came first and you had to guess how to keep it – there weren't any rules. How she had worried because there weren't any rules, reading everything she could find about the saints, trying to discover the secret. She never could have lasted long, that was certain. Still, she looked back at a spell of tranquil weather, the calm that came when she touched the book. She didn't remember reading that one, but she might have, or the word *Saints* on the cover had been enough to bring back the calm of the season.

So now she knew. It was religion, after all. How sad. She felt in her bag for the book, feeling nothing as she touched it but melancholy. She had told herself, you have to know, and had exchanged a useful spell for something she knew already, that religion made you happy. Of course it made you happy; that wasn't the point.

Where was she going? She was halfway down the main street, past the park. Her feet were taking her home from school.

After all, why not? Might as well do the thing thoroughly, go and look at the house and maybe lay a ghost or two. She was going undefended, since virtue had gone out of the book, but the whole place looked so empty, so peaceful, she felt she could risk it. She took the familiar turning, though it was no longer familiar. Estrangement. She climbed a hill, crossed a road, descended, turned, climbed again. There was the house, dead as a dead tooth. She stood and waited for something, anything, felt only blankness. She walked on.

A voice called, 'Isobel! Isobel!'

Run, Isobel, run! You put a lady's name in the paper, Isobel. She's going to have you put in jail. We can't save you; you should have asked Mummy, you should have asked Daddy. Run, Isobel, run! Run and hide!

Too late. Too late to run past, head down and heart banging. Caught. She forced her face towards the woman who was coming down her front path to the gate – such a tiny little woman that Isobel in her big quaking body felt like Alice after she had been at the magic drink. Drink me. She could do with a few of the cakes, right now.

Mrs Adams. Mrs Adams lives three doors from me. Mrs Adams was coming towards her, smiling. Could she have forgotten? Mrs Adams the bogeyman, bogeywoman, was coming towards her smiling brightly.

'Well, Isobel. Fancy seeing you. What are you doing with yourself now?'

'Working.' She stopped to steady her breathing. 'I'm working in an importer's office in town.'

'That's nice. And how is Margaret? Does she like it in the country?'

'Yes. She likes it very much. She's very well.'

'I am glad. Such a dear little girl. You're not in a hurry, are you? Come in and have a cup of tea.'

Oh no, Mrs Adams, it's a trap. You'll call the police to put me in jail.

What rubbish it was. Of course you didn't go to jail for putting a lady's name in the paper – certainly not at the age of nine. Still, she had to force herself to follow Mrs Adams down the narrow dim hall into the bright kitchen. The ignorance of her parents, and the years of misery it had caused her! Years of terror: doing the messages, she had bolted past the house in a frenzy of fear, getting past unseen, usually, but when Mrs Adams had seen her and called her, how she had run, till her legs went to jelly and her breath hurt her lungs.

In the confessional, she had whispered, 'I put a lady's name in the paper.' 'That's not a sin.' Not a sin; no hope, then, no absolution.

'Sit down while I put the kettle on,' Mrs Adams said.

The smell of gas and breadcrumbs, polish over mould, just like their own place, was getting to her, taking her back as the sight of the house hadn't done. She thought, I always expected to be happy, getting home. Never learnt from experience.

Mrs Adams got down cups, put tea in the teapot and biscuits on a plate, then said, 'Now, wait a minute. There's something I want to show you.'

She went out and came back carrying a photograph album, set it open on the table in front of Isobel and pointed to a photograph of a cat, with a newspaper cutting pasted below it.

'I don't suppose you remember that, do you? Dear old Smoke. Do you take milk, Isobel?'

'No, thank you.'

She was reading , her face burning and her head buzzing like a bee in the sunlight.

> Mrs Adams lives three doors from me.
> She has a cat. Smoke is his name.
> He curls around the corner silently.
> When he jumps, his name should be Flame.
>
> Blue Certificate to Isobel Callaghan (9 years).

While she was reading a lot of things came back.

There's a writer in there, Isobel; a naked infant greased

and trussed in the baking-dish with an apple jammed in its mouth.

Mrs Prendergast knew all about it. Mrs Prendergast's weird world was the true one. 'I won't be a minute, dear. I'm just popping the baby in the oven.'

Mrs Adams said, 'I was so thrilled with that little poem of yours. Everybody telling me Smoke was a silly name for a cat. That was just the way he walked and I called him Smoke because of that, not the colour, though that came into it a bit. I didn't see the poem myself; my niece's little girl – well, she's not a little girl any longer, she's the same age as you – well, she cut it out to show me, and my niece said to me, 'Well, what do you know, Smoke's famous!'

'Dear old Smoke, he lived to be ten and I miss him still. I often think, it's the little poem that brings him back, more than the photograph. I was so pleased, I bought you a book to paste your poems in, and a snap of Smoke, but you used to run away whenever I called you. You were a shy little thing, weren't you? I asked your mother to give it to you, but she said it would encourage you to waste time away from your school work. I suppose that was only right.' Right or not, Mrs Adams frowned over it slightly.

No, they wouldn't want a writer about the house. A witness, a recorder. Now you'll show all your poems to Mummy, won't you? No hope left when she started calling herself Mummy.

Isobel mumbled, 'I thought you were angry . . . becauseIputyournameinthe – paper . . .'

'Whatever made you think that?' Seeing the answer, she retreated quickly, murmuring, 'A strange woman in some ways.'

'Do you still have the book. The book you were going to give me?'

'No. Oh, dear, I am sorry. If I'd thought you wanted

it! I gave it to my niece to paste her recipes in.'

Observing that, somehow or other, she had drunk her cup of tea, Isobel got up. 'It was very nice of you to think of it, just the same. I'm sorry Smoke died. He was a beautiful cat.'

'Well, nothing lasts for ever, as they say.'

I hope they are right, Mrs Adams.

'You won't have another cup?'

She shook her head. She had to get out, fast, because she was coming to pieces, in great slabs, in chunks, like an iceberg breaking up. She said thinly, 'No, thank you. I'll have to be going.'

Mrs Adams ushered her into the street, which was almost as unsuitable as the house for the tears that were coming. Artesian tears, rising from the centre of the earth. Where could she go to shed them?

Bastards, bastards, bastards. Cruel, deceitful bastards.

She hurried along the street; behind the last few houses there was a rocky slope too steep for building. She went downhill to the street below and turned back, ran scrambling upwards, found the rock that she remembered and crouched behind it. Then she roared aloud, 'Spiteful tormenting bastards.' Her father, too. She used to delude herself that her father had loved her, seeing that he had died too soon to disprove it, but it wasn't so, he had been just as bad, with his pompous talk about libel and slander – libel and slander, for God's sake, the woman owned a *cat*. Run and hide, Isobel, here she comes. Here comes Mrs Adams!

The tears were coming slowly. How could tears come from so deep, as if she was a tree with tears welling up from its roots? Then they came in a roaring flood that drowned thought; she put her cheek against the rock, which was as rough as a cat's tongue and unyielding, but she was too far gone to feel any perverse pleasure in that. Her sobs were so loud that even in this wasteland she had to put her hands over her mouth to muffle them; when her mind sobered up her body went on snuffling and heaving along ten years of roadway.

I am a writer. I am a writer.

Too late. It must be too late. The poor little bugger in the baking dish; nobody came in time.

Suppose I tried? Suppose I went through the motions? The writer might come back.

You've tried that with love. It doesn't work.

But that was other people, too. This is me.

The crying had slackened. There was such a feeling of limbs stretching, of hands unbound, she knew she could choose to be a writer. A pen and an exercise book, that was all it took, to be a rotten writer, anyhow. Good or rotten, that came later.

It meant giving in to the word factory. That frightened her, because the word factory was such a menace. Now she understood why the idea of being press-ganged was so alarming.

Oh, well. If you can't lick 'em join 'em.

Maybe that was what the word factory was all about, the poor little bugger trying to get out of the baking dish.

She giggled and that was the end of the crying. It was getting dark and she was cold in her thin blouse and skirt. She got up, scrambled down the rocky slope with drying tears stinging on her face, her drenched handkerchief stuffed into her pocket and soaking through to the skin. She stood in the darkening street brushing her skirt and trying to tidy her hair with her fingers, cold, peckish, uncomfortable and utterly happy.

Where could she buy an exercise book at this time on Sunday? She would have to walk to the main street, unless there was a corner shop still open. It was wonderful to have a problem just that size, something to walk up a street for, instead of drifting like an escaped balloon.

She was so absorbed in her thoughts she nearly walked past the dim light that combed through the bead curtain at the open door of the little shop. The man behind the counter gave her a funny look – no wonder, she thought, looking into the spotted mirror that advertised Fulton's Orangeade. Behind the lettering she saw herself, wild-haired, blubbered, red-eyed, and thought, This is the happiest moment of my life.

The shopkeeper brought her the exercise book; she groped for her purse and touched the book. That was a moment, when she exchanged one talisman for another.

She said, 'Don't bother to wrap it,' dropped the exercise book into her bag beside the book and went out.

In the garden opposite, an untidy palm tree stood clumped against the fading pastels of the sky, and that was all right, too.

Back in her room at last, she opened the exercise book (this moment will never come again) and wrote at the top of the first page:

The Book is Gone

'*Now see this. I open my eyes and there's a girl – naked, not a stitch on her –* '

'*Half your luck.*'

'*Oh well. I'd had my luck, if you call it that. She was a left-over from last night, but what was she doing? Sitting with her bum on her heels in front of my bookcase reading Plato.*'

'*So you said . . .*'

'*What's a nice girl like you doing in a place like this? No, I didn't. Though I suppose it was what she was waiting for.*'

'*Mean bastard, aren't you?*'

'I could have been meaner, could have asked her for a few words on philosophy. Instead, I made light of it, tried to jolly her into putting her clothes on – damn it, she'd had plenty of time to get dressed – what the hell are you grinning at?'

'Your sense of sin. Reading Plato with no clothes on.'

'Well, now you come to mention it, I did think it was cheek.'

'The Greeks weren't so fussy.'

'Well, this is what's funny. I went and had a shower, and when I came back, she was gone and – this is it – so was the book.'

'And her clothes? Do tell!'

'Of course her clothes.'

'Oh blast. You just ruined a beautiful image.'

No, not Plato. Plato was too obvious. Something to get the second young man guessing, building up a whole skeleton from a toebone, nagging the first one about it. You can see he's haunted by the image of a naked girl reading . . . Turgenev?

She put down her pen and bit at her thumbnail, not for the last time.

The book must go, of course, back to Michael. She would wrap it and leave it in his letter box. She was sad to think of parting with it, but she could live without it. There were words to carry as talismans.

'Did you have a good weekend, Isobel?'

Christ, was that just a weekend?

I met the ghosts of two murderers when I was out for a walk, found the semi-strangled body of an infant learning to talk . . .

For a moment she felt threatened, seeing the walls of the word factory coming in on her, but she rallied.

Take it down, consider it later. The boy who had chased her and then couldn't hit her, make a note.

'Very nice, thanks.'

She smiled so happily that Rita said, 'I do believe our Isobel has met someone.'

Oh, yes.

Uncovering her typewriter, Isobel greeted it with a warm private smile.

Oh, yes, she thought joyfully. I met someone.

FOR THE BEST PAPERBACKS, LOOK FOR THE

PENGUIN

BOOKS BY JESSICA ANDERSON in Penguin
Stories from the Warm Zone and Sydney Stories

Jessica Anderson's evocative stories recreate, through the eyes of a child, the atmosphere of Australia between the wars. A stammer becomes a blessing in disguise; the prospect of a middle name converts a reluctant child to baptism. These autobiographical stories of a Brisbane childhood glow with the warmth of memory.

The formless sprawl of Sydney in the 1980s is a very different world. Here the lives of other characters are changed by the uncertainties of divorce, chance meetings and the disintegration and generation of relationships.

Winner of The Age Book of the Year Award.

Tirra Lirra by the River

A beautifully written novel of a woman's seventy-year search to find a place where she truly belongs.

For Nora Porteous, life is a series of escapes. To escape her tightly knit small-town family, she marries, only to find herself confined again, this time in a stifling Sydney suburb with a selfish, sanctimonious husband. With a courage born of desperation and sustained by a spirited sense of humour, Nora travels to London, and it is there that she becomes the woman she wants to be. Or does she?

FOR THE BEST PAPERBACKS, LOOK FOR THE

PENGUIN

BOOKS BY THEA ASTLEY in Penguin
Hunting the Wild Pineapple

Leverson the narrator, at the centre of these stories, calls himself a 'people freak'. Seduced by north Queensland's sultry beauty and unique strangeness, he is as fascinated by the invading hordes of misfits from the south as by the old-established Queenslanders.

Leverson's ironical yet compassionate view makes every story, every incident, a pointed example of human weakness – or strength.

It's Raining in Mango

Sometimes history repeats itself.

One family traced from the 1860s to the 1980s: from Cornelius to Connie to Reever, who was last seen heading north.

Cornelius Laffey, an Irish–born journalist, wrests his family from the easy living of nineteenth-century Sydney and takes them to Cooktown in northern Queensland where thousands of diggers are searching for gold in the mud. The family confront the horror of Aboriginal dispossession – Cornelius is sacked for reporting the slaughter. His daughter, Nadine, joins the singing whore on the barge and goes upstream, only to be washed out to sea.

The cycles of generations turn, one over the other. Only some things change. That world and this world both have their Catholic priests, their bigots, their radicals. Full of powerful and independent characters, this is an unforgettable tale of the other side of Australia's heritage.

FOR THE BEST PAPERBACKS, LOOK FOR THE

PENGUIN

BOOKS BY ELIZABETH JOLLEY in Penguin
The Sugar Mother

An aging but handsome university professor, Edwin Page, is married to Cecilia, a much younger woman who is an obstetrician and gynaecologist. (He was attracted to her in the first place by all the mysterious things she knew about the human body.) When the childless Cecilia goes away for a year's study leave, Edwin finds himself more and more in the company of Leila and her mother who live next door. Leila's mother is a very good cook, and Leila, it turns out, is perfectly willing to be a surrogate mother . . .

The Sugar Mother explores the way the many little impacts of distance, separation and change can gather force and move people in unexpected directions. It is a witty, disturbing story of self–deception and of hopes, perhaps secret hopes.

Mr Scobie's Riddle

Mr Scobie's arrival at the nursing home of St Christopher and St Jude – and into the clutches of Matron Hyacinth Price – is accidental. Self-educated and still preserving the gift of idyllic memory and wish, Mr Scobie stands apart from the others. For long-term resident and eccentric, Miss Haily, he represents a kindred spirit; for Matron Price – a lady of questionable practices – the latest victim . . .

But unwittingly Mr Scobie has some recourse – his very simple riddle. Its answer – an ancient commonplace – jolts Matron Price.

Yet it is Mr Scobie's nephew, Hartley, and the group of nocturnal poker players, who ultimately change Matron Price's establishment . . .

FOR THE BEST PAPERBACKS, LOOK FOR THE 🐧

PENGUIN

Steel Beach
Margaret Barbalet

The view from the house distracted me from my work. Held between the beach and the escarpment, I would look up from my papers and my eye would take in the sweep of the coastline – the same coastline that Lawrence and Frieda had explored half a century before. Now I was the explorer, mapping out the life they had led there.

I met a surfer on the beach yesterday who was the image of Lawrence. As soon as I saw him, I knew he was important. He was my first clue.

FOR THE BEST PAPERBACKS, LOOK FOR THE (🐧)

PENGUIN

Miracle of the Waters
Zeny Giles

They come from the edges of the continent, inland, seeking comfort in the waters that bubble out from the earth's warm core.

Joining the small but devoted band of locals are Greeks, Czechs, Turks, Hungarians, lovers and the unloved, dreamers and cynics, the weary, the wasting and the wanton.

In illuminating the emotional and cultural dislocation of people, brought together in Australia by the tradition of 'taking the waters' at the Moree Hot Baths, Zeny Giles' collection of stories evokes simply but powerfully how much is common in a world full of differences.

FOR THE BEST PAPERBACKS, LOOK FOR THE

PENGUIN

The Hanged Man in the Garden
Marion Halligan

'. . . the Hanged Man dangles gallantly by one foot and turning upside down observes the world. Its powers cannot harm him, he sees it clearly and afresh, all new. He is an individual. And he has a halo round his head.'

The Hanged Man represents a turn–around of perception that often occurs when an individual confronts pain. A baby dies, a husband is unfaithful, a woman spends a week in a cupboard, people strive to come to terms with grief and loss – variously they choose humour, despair, irony and hope. It is the unexpectedness of this illogical reversal that makes the experience precious. And, how ever hard life may be, the sensuous beauty of its surfaces is a source of pleasure.

One of Australia's foremost short–story writers, Marion Halligan explores, through the interweaving lives of a group of individuals, the complexities of pain.

FOR THE BEST PAPERBACKS, LOOK FOR THE

PENGUIN

The Glass Whittler
Stephanie Johnson

A young woman changes cities, but no one in the new city needs a glass whittler; Robyn, a single mother, buys a house on the proceeds of an unusual business; Nola is fat – one night, reminded of the joys of chocolate by the television she decides to go out – but Nola is locked inside her flat and cannot get out; a retired schoolmistress who has had a stroke is cared for by an alcoholic tramp who has made himself at home in her flat.

Twelve stories by a remarkable young writer. Stephanie Johnson writes about craving for love and companionship, for security and the approval of others. The people in these stories seem to find unusual ways of coping with the absurdities and constraints of modern life. But perhaps their solutions are not so strange.